The Switching Hour

Damaris Young

SCHOLASTIC

Scholastic Children's Books
An imprint of Scholastic Ltd
Euston House, 24 Eversholt Street, London, NW1 1DB, UK
Registered office: Westfield Road, Southam, Warwickshire, CV47 0RA
SCHOLASTIC and associated logos are trademarks and/or
registered trademarks of Scholastic Inc.

First published in the UK by Scholastic Ltd, 2019

ISBN 978 1407 19504 9

A CIP catalogue record for this book
is available from the British Library.

Printed by CPI Group (UK) Ltd, Croydon, CR0 4YY

Papers used by Scholastic Children's Books are made
from wood grown in sustainable forests.

1 3 5 7 9 10 8 6 4 2

www.scholastic.co.uk

To Mum and Dad

Chapter One

"The clouds have lost their way"

I dived down into the dark part of the water.

Like the eels had taught me, I twist-turned into the murky depths. Into the swish and sway of lake reeds, the green stalks whisper-soft against my skin, the air ballooning in my chest.

I searched for a rock with my feet. With my toes, I clamped on tight, while I unhooked the net from my weighted belt. I made slow, small movements, careful not to ripple the cold water.

A flash of silver in the shadows and I had the lake bream in my sights. A single fish.

With a flick of my wrist, I spun the net and closed it tight, the small fish entangled and fighting inside. *Finally.*

Holding the net with both hands, I shot up towards

the surface, where I spat out lake water with its grit and fishy taste and pulled clean air into my lungs.

I squinted upwards to read the sun. It'd fallen towards the west, but it was still hot enough to suck the water off my face. I swam closer to the shoreline and reached down to the bottom of the lake until my toes dug into mud. The net grew heavy as I walked out of the water.

My pet goat greeted me with a wriggle of his tail. He headbutted me hard enough to almost tip me back into the lake.

"Careful, Tau!" I scolded.

He'd kept himself busy while I'd been fishing. Green moss poked out of the corner of his beard. He must have climbed the boulders that lined the lake, to get to the plants that grew in the crevices. There was so little else to eat since the drought had taken over our once-green country, leaving it cracked and parched.

I searched the sky for clouds. Even a whisper of haze could be enough to mean the rains were here at last, but there was nothing beyond the great and empty blue.

"The clouds have lost their way," I said to Tau. "Maybe tomorrow, the rains will find us."

Nearby, a spadefoot croaked from its burrow hole. The toads liked the cool of the evening; I heard the impatience in its voice.

My cotton tunic was hanging on a needle-thorn tree and I pulled it on without waiting for my skin to dry. My curly hair dripped water, so I shook my head until I felt dizzy.

The spadefoot croaked again. Louder this time. Then more toads joined in, until the rattle of their song almost shook the earth under my feet.

It would soon be the Switching Hour, where day traded places with the night.

A panic-flutter woke up in my stomach.

"Let's go home, Tau!" I called out with a fierceness that I knew he understood. We were running out of time.

The fish bucket bumped against my legs as I ran through the long, yellow grass. It grew as high as my shoulder, and I stomped my feet to scare away the orange-bellied snakes that liked to hide there.

I raced Tau along the path, skittering stones beneath my feet, until we got to the pastures where two older goats grazed.

Zola, the colour of milk. Ela, the colour of honey.

I whistled with two fingers in my mouth, shrill as the shriek of an egret.

The goats trotted over, kicking up dust. The grazing grass had all but gone.

Tau danced around them, just out of range of Zola's huge curved horns.

"We have to hurry!" I said. I threaded twine through their leather collars and pulled them into a walk.

"Through the gate, Zola," I coaxed, leading them on.

Faster! I willed them, but goats are stubborn creatures and will only go as quickly as they want. I tugged on the twine and tried to get them both into a trot.

The Switching Hour had begun. The sun was setting behind the forest when I caught sight of smoke curling upwards from behind a thicket of needle-thorn trees, their branches black against the sky. It was almost dark now and I could already see the first pinpricks of stars.

The rising tide of night had washed away the day.

Granny Uma was waiting for me by the cottage door.

"You're late, Amaya!" she said, her voice scratched with worry. She grabbed the harness rope out of my hand and pushed me towards the open door and safety.

Chapter Two

"You're lucky to be on this side of the door"

While Granny Uma locked Zola and Ela in the goat shed, I sneaked Tau into the cottage. After being outside all day, the smell of the paraffin lamps made my nose twitch.

Tau went straight to the rug near the hearth and curled up. He snuffled and closed his eyes.

"Lazy goat," I muttered, tweaking his tail.

I dropped the fish bucket on to the table with a thump.

A chuckling noise sounded from under the table. I peeked underneath. Kaleb sat plump and upright on the kitchen floor, gnawing on a rind of pumpkin skin. He dropped it as soon as he saw me looking and stretched upwards, clenching and unclenching his hands.

7

I bent down and picked him up, pretending to groan with the weight of him.

"You're getting fat on pumpkin, small brother. Soon, you'll turn into a pumpkin yourself!" I squeezed him tight and he laughed.

Kaleb had a whooping laugh, full of belly sound, and he smelled of trampled grass and soil. I wiped the dirt from his hands.

"You need a bath," I said as he wriggled out of my arms.

The cottage door closed with enough force to shake the dust from the thatch.

Even with her grey hair and tired eyes, Granny Uma was the toughest person I knew. It's better to just get out of her way when she's angry.

I went to latch up the windows. Locking the outside out.

It didn't take long. There was only one window in each of the three rooms, all set deep into the thick stone walls. Once the windows were secured, I went and stood next to Granny Uma, ready for the door-locking routine.

Granny Uma turned the heavy key until the lock clunked into position. She left it in place so that it stuck out of the door like a silver arrow.

"Now make sure the deadbolt is secured." She muttered the words to herself like an incantation, shoving the bolt along its fixture. Its squeak made my teeth itch.

Granny Uma turned to face me.

"Check it's locked, Amaya," she said. "Always make sure the door is secured."

I can see it is, why should I have to check it? I thought, but I did what she said. I rattled the door handle, turning it this way and that.

"It's locked."

"Would you stake your life on it?" I could sense Granny Uma's eyes boring into me. I glared at the door.

"Yes. Definitely."

Granny Uma had insisted on this nightly routine ever since the wells had started to dry up and the drought had taken hold. It always felt silly to keep checking the door when I knew it was shut tight.

It was just another thing to get used to, since me and Kaleb had moved in with her.

I stifled a yawn and Granny Uma shot me a look with dagger-sharp eyes. Her hair had untied itself from her braid.

"You're lucky to be on this side of the door, Amaya. You left it very late."

"I'm sorry."

"It's not enough to be sorry. You know the dangers, you're twelve summers old." Granny Uma's voice splintered into an almost-sob that hurt more than words could. "What if you hadn't made it back in time?"

I could only look at the floor.

"Do you think it's a game, staying out as late as you want?" she said. "Badeko will snatch you away if you're not careful!"

"I waited until the others had left the lake. So many people fish there now that there's hardly any fish left. It's easier to catch them when it's quiet," I said. But no matter how hungry we were, I knew Granny Uma wouldn't care about the fish. It wasn't a good enough excuse.

The drought had awoken Badeko. A creature that stole away children at night, to eat their dreams. You had to make sure you were safely behind locked doors after the Switching Hour, otherwise you'd become its prey.

Or so Granny Uma said. Mama had whispered that it was just a story.

Granny Uma clicked her tongue.

"Help me with supper," she said. "And don't waste time bringing the goats home if you're late. Your life is far more precious than a goat's."

I glanced at Tau, curled up next to the fire. He looked like a mud ball, his white fur all dirty. When Ela rejected him for being birthed sickly small, I had loved him and raised him up strong.

"Hurry, Amaya!" Granny Uma called over from the kitchen table.

From the bucket, I grabbed the bream and laid it out on the wooden board on the table. Selecting the filleting knife, I carved the fish open in one smooth movement.

The insides spilled out. I slopped the pink and white wormlike entrails into the chum bucket. The knife was sharp, and I chopped off the dead-eyed head with one slice. I quickly closed the wooden top of the bucket, so that the smell wouldn't fill the room.

I cut the fish into thumb-sized chunks that would cook easily. I wiped the knife with the washcloth before putting it back in the high-up wood block, away from Kaleb's grabbing hands.

Fish scales glittered like pearl dust under my

fingernails. I waggled them at Kaleb, but he tried to bite my fingers.

"Leave my fingers in one piece!" I laughed. "Chomp on your pumpkin instead."

All of his tiny teeth had shoved their way out of his gums, and he gnawed on anything he could grab. Tau had learned to stay out of his way.

"The stew is bubbling," Granny Uma said. "Bring the fish over, Amaya."

She dipped a ladle into the iron pot on the stove and slurped a taste. She tutted. "More pepper."

While Granny Uma crushed up a pepper clove, I carried the fish pieces over to the pot and tossed them in, watching them disappear under the stew-skin.

"Is that enough stew, Granny Uma?" It barely covered the bottom of the large iron pot.

"There's porridge to go with it." The thick, gloopy liquid spluttered in a pot on the other hob. Granny Uma sprinkled pepper into the stew, the powerful smell swirling with the steam, masking the stink of paraffin.

"So the lake was busy today?" she asked.

I nodded. "Too many people. Not enough fish." I slammed the empty board on to the table, making Tau jump in his sleep.

Granny Uma wiped her hands on her apron. "Amaya, the lake is for everyone. The drought affects all things. People, animals, the birds and the trees all suffer. Only by working together can we survive."

"The lake levels are lower than yesterday," I said pointedly. The well had started to draw silt along with the water; it wouldn't be long until it dried up completely unless the rains appeared soon.

Granny Uma sucked her teeth. She didn't say anything more about it, but her mouth went taut as a fishing line.

I searched for Kaleb. He'd clambered up on the stool, stretching for the stew ladle.

"Come here, pumpkin boy!" I picked him up and lugged him over to the fireside, where I sat down on the hearth rug and leaned against Tau's warm side, his snores rumbling against my back.

Kaleb wanted to get my bracelet off my wrist, so I unhooked it and dangled it above him. He laughed, reaching up to try and catch it.

I'd made it with wool dyed blue, green and black. The colours of the sky and the grasslands, and black for the forest that bordered the fields where Zola and Ela grazed.

Granny Uma passed me two bowls of stew and porridge.

My stomach grumbled. There was barely enough in the bowls to feed a mouse.

I blew on a spoonful before giving it to Kaleb. I couldn't help laughing as he chomped on the wooden spoon with his new teeth, his face scrunched up in concentration.

The wicker chair creaked as Granny Uma sat down.

"When you didn't come home, I thought Badeko had taken you away. Do you want me to suffer the loss of my only granddaughter as well as my daughter?" Her voice cracked and she hacked a cough.

"I'm sorry," I said, and this time I meant it.

Granny Uma missed Mama as much as we did. She hadn't cried in front of us in the months that me and Kaleb had been living with her, but I'd heard her sobs in the middle of the night when I couldn't sleep. I'd always cover my head with the pillow, to try and block out all the sadness. It never worked.

"Until the rains arrive," Granny Uma said, "you *must* come home before the Switching Hour. No one is safe from Badeko the Dream Eater at night, no matter how fast you think you can run."

The logs shifted in the hearth, making me jump. As the wood crumbled, sparks whirled up the chimney.

I pulled Kaleb on to my lap, his back nestled against my chest, and I watched Granny Uma carefully. The firelight smoothed out the crags in her face. She looked like Mama.

"Mama told me Badeko was just a myth," I said under my breath, but Granny Uma heard me just fine.

"Your mama hadn't experienced a drought before."

"Do you remember the last time the Dream Eater woke up?" I asked her.

Granny Uma shook her head. "It was before my time. The Great Drought of a hundred years ago." She sucked on her teeth, a habit she had when she was storytelling. The sucking sound was as much a part of the story as the words. "The story of Badeko was passed down from my mama and hers before that." She smoothed out the cross-stitched shawl that was draped over her legs. It had been made by her grandmama. "The stories are gifts, given to us by those that love us, who wish to warn us of what lurks in the dark. It will be your responsibility to pass it on as well, when the time comes."

Kaleb yawned in my lap. I rested my chin gently on his head, smelling the earth that clung to his hair and the fire-warmth on his skin.

"Tell me about Badeko, Granny Uma," I asked her.

Granny Uma sucked her teeth and her eyes darkened.

"When the rivers dry up, the Dream Eater awakens from its nest under the Dead Tree, hidden in the middle of the forest. It roams the night-time world, using its trickery to lure people out of their houses. Never let it in," she said. "If you are caught, it will take you to the tree that's white as bones. Once there, it will sing a song to send you into a sleep that you cannot wake from."

I glanced towards the locked door, fear rising through me. "What happens then?"

"As Badeko eats your dreams with its sharp teeth, the memory of your unfortunate soul begins to disappear from the minds of those that knew and loved it – no one will remember you enough to attempt a rescue. Your family and friends will catch the Sorrow Sickness and be cursed to grieve for someone they can't remember."

"You're scaring Kaleb," I said, even though my heart thumped the loudest. In my lap, Kaleb rubbed his eyes with a closed fist, struggling to stay awake, while Tau continued to snore softly.

"It only takes three days for the Sorrow Sickness to claim you," Granny Uma continued without looking away from the fire. "Five children from the Forest Settlement have already been taken and their families are weighed down by the fog of grief." She exhaled. "It could be our house next. Wherever there are dreamers, the creature will find them."

Granny Uma tightened her lips. She was done talking.

My arm ached with holding up Kaleb's head – he had fallen soundly asleep. In the firelight, his long eyelashes made shadows on his skin, while his eyes flickered under their lids. I wondered what he was dreaming of.

Granny Uma heaved herself out of her chair. "Time for bed, Amaya."

I carried Kaleb to his wooden cot and put him down, pulling the wool blanket over him. I placed my hand gently on his chest and felt the rise and fall of his sleeping breath.

Quietly, I sang him the bedtime rhyme that Mama had sung to me. It seemed to help Kaleb sleep so I still sang it each night, even though hearing her voice in the words made the pain of missing her worse.

> *Close your eyes and breathe in deep*
> *It's time for you to go to sleep*
> *Until the moon has gone to hide*
> *I will be right by your side.*

I tiptoed to my bed and snuggled under the cover.

After Mama had died and we'd come to live with Granny Uma, I'd begged her to let Kaleb sleep in my room instead of hers. I told her that if he woke up in the night, I could be there for him, but he always slept through until morning.

It was me who would wake, fighting the nightmares that crept into the room at night, memories of smoke and heat and screams. Whenever it was really bad and I was stuck, frozen between the dream and waking, I'd focus on the sound of Kaleb's quiet breathing, until the nightmare let me go.

The bed creaked as Tau jumped on to the end of it, squashing my legs under the blanket. The weight of him there was comforting, even if he smelled of old yams and mash.

"Goodnight, Kaleb. Goodnight, Tau," I whispered into the darkened room.

Chapter Three

"Never let the outside in"

The night was at its darkest point. Out of the forest crept a creature with lichen skin and as it sniffed the air, its milk-white eyes blinked. It caught a scent and scuttled on its many legs through the dead, dry grass, following the fragrance of sleep and dreams.

The house stood quiet. The creature leaned down to the gap under the door, licking the air with a lizard tongue. The Old One slept nearby and the creature tasted the tang of long-ago memories, flavours of pumpkin and wool. It searched the air for more. The creature could taste burned wood, scorched earth and ash. The girl who dreamed of fire was there.

Its belly rumbled and the creature breathed in deep, until finally its tongue tingled with the zest of new grass, warm milk and sorghum biscuits. The small boy dreamed too.

The creature licked its lips and sucked the dream through its sharp teeth, but the empty hunger in its belly still roared. It wasn't enough. Always hungry. Always thirsty.

I awoke with a start.

My hair and pillow were damp with sweat. I felt it drip, spider-like, down my skin. I caught snatches of my dream before it disappeared. I'd dreamed of Mama again, the memory fluttering helplessly like a moth trapped between a pair of hands. I'd tried to get into our old house as smoke had pushed against the window, but the door had been locked from the inside.

As the nightmare faded, I could still taste charcoal grit in my mouth.

Why is dreaming so exhausting? I would give anything to have one dreamless sleep.

Even though the room was dark, Kaleb's soft breathing made me feel less alone. I stretched out and reached for Tau. Curled up at the end of my bed, he grumbled as I tickled his back, but he didn't wake up.

Closing my eyes, I tried to drift off again, but I couldn't shake the feeling there had been something else that had woken me.

I sat up and pulled off the blanket that had

become entangled in my legs. I always kicked out fiercely when I had nightmares. Sometimes Granny Uma shook me awake if I was calling out.

But not tonight. Her snores could be heard from the other room.

I listened, breathing quietly.

There were the usual night noises. The skitter of a mouse across the roof beams, and the cricket hum from outside. A churring call of a nightjar sounded from the needle-thorn thicket. *Is that what had woken me?*

I eased myself out of bed and crept over to Kaleb's crib. I peered in. My brother slept peacefully, his arms and legs sprawled across the mattress.

I turned to go back to bed.

Then I heard it.

A sound from outside the cottage door.

Frozen in place, I listened over my hammering heartbeat.

Something was crying. But it wasn't the sound of an animal.

"A baby!" I whispered in the dark.

I stepped silently across the room, feeling every lump and bump of the floor under my bare feet.

The baby cried out again.

Granny Uma's bedroom door was open and I peeked inside.

The bed creaked and she mumbled in her sleep but she didn't wake.

I turned away. Careful not to make any sound, I crept past the kitchen and into the main room where the fire had burnt down to embers, the glow casting shapes against the far wall. My shadow followed me across the room.

I reached the cottage door and stopped.

The crying grew louder, as if the baby *knew* I was nearby. My chest squeezed at the misery in its small voice. I thought of Kaleb. When he cried, I always ran to him and picked him up. I kissed the hurt away and wiped his tears.

Should I open the door?

But Granny Uma had told me not to. I'd promised her.

While I tried to decide what to do, a humming sound, like rain on the ground, seeped in from under the door, drowning out the crying. It was a beautiful song without words that soaked into my skin, tingling and warm. I could feel every hair on my arms stand up. The urge to open the door grew stronger. *Maybe I could peek outside?*

I reached for the bolt, the metal cold against my fingers.

Never let the outside in! I remembered Granny Uma's warning.

With my hand on the latch, I paused.

I leaned my head against the wood of the door.

My heart beat *thud thud thud* in my ear.

No baby cry.

No humming song.

But something else, a different sound. A scratch and scritch against the grain of the door. Nails against wood.

Claws.

I snatched my hand away from the bolt as if my fingers had been licked by flame. I moved across the floor on lightning feet and over to the shutters.

Although the window was barred with three heavy wooden beams, there were cracks between each one, enough to see out. I peered through the gap.

The moon was only a slice and the stars seemed even further away than normal tonight. Dawn would not break for hours. The path led from the cottage to the closed garden gate, through grass that grew black and blue in the night-time light.

Was there something in the needle-thorn tree, sitting

in the crook of the branch? I couldn't tell, but my skin felt bloodless cold.

A shiver prickled down my spine. *Kaleb!*

I ran to the cot and leaned in. He slept soundly. Gently, I placed my hand on his chest and felt the warmth from his skin through the wool blanket.

"The door is locked. We're safe," I murmured, quiet enough not to wake Granny Uma or Kaleb. I considered what could have made the noise outside. *It must have been the shriek of an owl or the wind in the needle-thorn tree.*

I crept back to my bed. But sleep only came in slithers and snatches. Every time I drifted off I thought I heard the humming song, only for it to fade away when I opened my eyes.

Chapter Four

"I'm not expecting any visitors today"

A rasping tongue woke me up. Something was snuffling at my face.

"Tau!" I groaned. With one eye open, I glared into the brown eyes of the goat, who was now nibbling my hair. I wiped the drool off my face.

I pushed him away, then kicked the blanket off my legs. The sun shone white-bright through the cracks in the shutters and dust specks swarmed in the slants of light.

I pulled on yesterday's clothes that were within reach on the floor. Embroidered with yellow weaving birds and purple flowers by Granny Uma, my tunic and trousers smelled of the lake, pondweed and mud. Something clattered to the floor.

"Mama's stone." I swooped it up. It fit perfectly

in my palm. The stone was the same colour as my mama's eyes, dark brown with gold flecks. I'd found it in the lake after she'd gone.

That day, I'd escaped the well-wishers who'd brought sickly treacle cakes, thinking they were helping but only filling the air with pointless words. I'd slipped away, leaving Granny Uma to deal with their chatter and Kaleb and his demands, feeling guilty but not enough to stay a moment longer inside.

Once at the lake, I'd swum down into the water, into the darkness. The stone had been there at the bottom of the lake, a flash of gold, waiting for me. A sign from Mama.

She would have wanted me to find it, to help me remember her.

Even with the stone, the fear of forgetting her was constantly on my mind. It made me feel sick with worry; the panic-beast that lived in my stomach.

I slipped the stone back into the pocket of my tunic and felt the weight of it against my heart.

The cottage door swung open.

"You're awake, sleep-snatcher!" Granny Uma said. She lugged a pail of Ela's milk through the door, with Kaleb wrapped in a blue shawl on her back. He flashed a toothy smile when he saw me and wriggled to be set free.

Granny Uma plonked the pail on to the table. The milk sloshed against the sides, smelling sweet. From the kitchen, I brought slices of bread over and piled them high, while Granny Uma cracked two eggs into the pan instead of three. The hens had started laying less.

Kaleb reached out towards the cup. "'ilk!" he demanded. He was slower at finding his words than his feet. Granny Uma said he would learn soon enough; we just had to keep talking to him.

"You want some milk, small brother?" I refilled the cup, noticing there was less milk than yesterday, and crouched down next to him. "Milk!" I said, pointing at the cup, but he just tried to grab it from my hands.

I helped him drink, but he still got milk all down his clean clothes. He grinned with a dripping white moustache.

"You're a messy mouse!" I tried to wipe his face with the edge of my tunic, but he squirmed out of the way. I herded him over to his chair at the table for breakfast. My stomach rumbled at the smell.

Granny Uma had fried the eggs in butter. They

sat wobbling next to yam mash and a bowl of boiled red cabbage, with the bread that Granny Uma had toasted.

I was about to tell her about the noise I'd heard last night, when there was a *bang-bang-bang* on the door.

Granny Uma frowned. "I'm not expecting any visitors today," she said.

The knocking got louder.

Granny Uma pushed her chair back and stood up.

"Don't break the door down! I'm on my way," she grumbled. She glanced longingly at her eggs, then opened the door wide.

A man stood on the threshold, sweat pouring off his face even in the early morning. I recognized him from the Forest Settlement – he passed by our house weekly on his way to buy supplies from the Town.

Granny Uma nodded in welcome. "Good morning, Luca! Come in, we're about to eat breakfast if you'd like to join us?"

He shook his head, not looking into the cottage at Kaleb or me. "It's Sadi, my wife. She's been in labour all night. There's something wrong with the baby; it's not appearing as it should."

"Then I must go with you immediately!" Granny

Uma said. She turned and grabbed her medicine bag that she kept near the door for emergencies. She also gathered bundles of freshly dried herbs, which were strung from the roof beams. She motioned for me to pick up Kaleb and follow her outside.

I wiped the egg off Kaleb's face with a washcloth and carried him out of the cottage, into the bright sunshine.

Granny Uma asked Luca, "Have you come from the Forest Settlement?"

Luca shook his head. "We moved the family to the Eastern Town yesterday, away from the Forest and the Dream Eater."

"Have you seen it?" The words escaped before I could stop them.

Granny Uma shushed me, but Luca didn't seem to mind me asking.

"I have only seen what it's done to others," Luca said. "It's broken families, changed people…" He struggled with the words. "Turning them into a nothingness, as if they're ghosts."

The Sorrow Sickness? Could it be real?

"How can they be cured?" I felt desperate to know more.

"That's enough, Amaya." Granny Uma's tone was sharp enough to cut off any more questions. I huffed in frustration.

"I assume you've brought the cart with you?" Granny Uma said to Luca. "I can't leave the children here by themselves. We will have to stay with you overnight and return tomorrow."

Luca ran his hands through his hair. "I only brought the horse. I didn't think to cart her up. It would have slowed us down!"

Beautiful with her shiny black coat, his horse stood patiently tied to our fence, even though she could have torn the wooden stakes right out of the ground with one toss of her huge head. She paid no attention to Tau, who was making a great show of bucking his legs in the air.

"She can carry two people, but not four!" Luca stared at Granny Uma with pleading eyes. I could see the fear in them. I wondered if he thought it was already too late.

"You don't have to worry about us, Granny Uma. It's only one night; I can take care of Kaleb." I stood up as straight as possible, with Kaleb wriggling in my arms.

Granny Uma glanced at Luca then back at me.

"I can't leave them. There's no one else to look after them!"

"You're the only person who can help." I could hear the tears in his voice. "The baby won't make it without you and my wife is also in danger."

"It's too risky, leaving them by themselves." Granny Uma tightened her scarf around her shoulders. She shook her head and a strand of grey hair fell loose from her braid. "They're only children, and with Badeko awake and hungry for dreams..."

"We'll be fine!" I said, smiling wide. But inside my stomach clenched. I'd never stayed in the cottage by myself before.

I'd never taken care of Kaleb alone.

His eyes wide and afraid, Luca looked like he was ready to pick Granny Uma up and carry her to his wife. "Please, there's no other midwife in Town!"

"We'll be fine, Granny Uma. You have to help the baby." Kaleb continued to wriggle in my arms but I held on to him tightly. "Mama wouldn't have minded me looking after Kaleb by myself. She would have wanted you to do everything you could to save the baby."

Secretly, I knew Mama would have been furious at the thought of me being left to look after Kaleb on my own, but Luca's baby needed Granny Uma more than we did right now. *One small untruth couldn't hurt?*

It worked. Granny Uma nodded; she'd made up her mind. "OK," she said. "Amaya, you are in charge. Remember to feed Kaleb, make sure he doesn't get into mischief. And above all else: keep the door locked at night!"

She tucked a loose curl back behind my ear then kissed me lightly on the forehead and Kaleb on the cheek. He reached for her necklace. I'd made it for her from dried pumpkin and clatterpod seeds. The gentle rattle they made was the music that followed her around.

Granny Uma untangled Kaleb's fingers. "Don't let the outside in," she said to me. "Don't let Badeko into the house!"

I nodded and smiled again, even though my stomach felt full of grass snakes, slither-sliding over one another. But I knew that without Granny Uma, the unborn baby might not see the world.

Luca helped Granny Uma up on to the back of the horse, and they set off at a trot. With one last glance over her shoulder, Granny Uma disappeared behind the needle-thorn trees.

A small shiver of excitement ran through me. I had the whole day to do whatever I wanted. No bossy Granny Uma telling me what to do.

I just had to look after my brother at the same time. *That shouldn't be too difficult, surely? He was only small after all.*

I looked down at Kaleb. He stared at me with his black eyes.

"What shall we do today?"

He squirmed to be put down and as soon as I set him loose, he ran off into the house and straight over to Tau's feed bowl. He shoved Tau away from it and plunged his hands into the warm mash. Tau bleated in concern.

"That's not your food, Kaleb!" I scolded, pulling him away from the bowl.

I soon discovered looking after a toddling child is not easy on your own. Like a baby goat, he climbed, broke and ate anything he could get his hands on and disappeared every time I turned to look at anything other than him.

I led Ela and Zola back towards the pasture, with Kaleb tied to my back with a shawl. But he wriggled and fussed to be put down.

"Kaleb!" I shouted when he kicked the backs of my legs with his bare feet. "You can walk on your own then!" I untied the shawl and swung him to the ground. With one hand holding Kaleb's and the other wrapped around Ela and Zola's rope, I had to walk at toddling pace.

By the time I got to the pasture gate, the sun was already high up above.

I unlatched the gate and the goats trotted in, kicking up red dust under their hooves. They snuffled at the yellow stalks of grass without much interest. At least we still had enough grain to feed them. For now.

I shoved the gate closed.

Kaleb let go of my hand. He set off further down the path, towards the lake.

"Stubborn as a goat," I muttered.

I followed close behind. Tau snatched mouthfuls of yellow grass from the side of the path and brown leaves from the shrubs, his jaw moving from side to side.

The heat stung my scalp and I could smell my skin burning as my shoulders absorbed the sun. I glanced upwards, but there were no clouds.

Kaleb picked up stones that caught his eyes, then

flung each one into the long grass, causing a stork to erupt into the air.

"Don't throw stones, Kaleb!" I scolded, knowing full well I liked to do the same on walks. I felt guilty for rebuking him, so I picked a yellow flower off a needle-thorn tree and handed it to him.

"Keep hold of that instead."

Kaleb immediately fed the flower to Tau, laughing as the goat tickled his hand with his rubbery lips.

I tutted at Kaleb, just like Granny Uma would to me.

Further along the path, I saw two figures approach from the direction of the lake. I took hold of Kaleb's hand and held it tight.

When they got closer, I recognized one of the local fishermen, Hal, and his son, Dakari, who was close to my age. I used to be part of the same group of friends as Dakari, when I'd lived in Town. We'd go to the lake and swim and stay out past the Switching Hour, even though we'd been warned about Badeko. Mama hadn't minded me staying out later. No one had taken the creature seriously back then; now it was all anyone could talk about.

Since the drought took hold and the children started going missing, none of my friends had been allowed out by themselves. I missed them.

"There's no fish," Dakari said in greeting. He dropped an empty bucket on to the ground with a rattle.

"No one has had any luck this morning," added Hal. "The bream have all gone."

My gut twisted. The lake had never run out of fish before.

"I know how much you have been relying on the lake for food, Amaya." Hal looked at me in concern. "I hope your family have stored enough to see you through the drought." He glanced behind me, taking in the dry pasture where Ela and Zola grazed. "At least you have the goats, if it comes to that."

I grabbed hold of Tau's collar with my free hand. "They're not food."

Hal shook his head. "They're just more mouths to feed."

"Our cow is still giving us milk," Dakari spoke quickly. I know how much he loved their cow, who he called Nettie. I hoped the rains would come soon.

"Granny Uma is helping to deliver a baby in the Eastern Town," I told them. "I'm sure she'll pick up food while she's there."

"No supply boats have made it back down the

river yet," Hal said. His eyes twitched upwards, searching for the sun, as if it might suddenly drop to the horizon. "I'd advise you to go home. Too many have caught the Sorrow Sickness."

"Can Dakari stay and play a while?" I desperately wanted to talk to someone who wasn't a toddling, a granny or a goat.

Dakari looked hopeful, but his father shook his head. "It's not safe."

Dakari sullenly picked up the bucket. "Bye, Amaya." He rolled his eyes at his father's back.

Please don't go! I felt a sharp pang of loneliness. It had been so long since I saw my friends.

I had so many questions for Dakari. Whether he had seen the Sorrow Sickness with his own eyes, or even Badeko itself, or if he'd heard the noise of a baby crying at night – but it was too late. They had already set off down the path, back towards the Town.

I heaved Kaleb on to my shoulders, holding on to his chubby legs as I pushed through the long grass. He kicked out at the stalks as we walked past, narrowly missing my face with his feet. I grimaced as he steadied himself with handfuls of my hair.

As we pushed through the scratchy stalks, I could

see the lake sparkling. My body tingled with the thought of plunging into the cold water.

The lake was deserted – word must have already spread that the fish had disappeared. The windmill that pumped water to the nearby fields had stopped, the water levels now too low.

The strangeness of the quiet felt exposing.

I lifted Kaleb off my shoulders and he toddled full pelt down towards the water. Tau bounded around him like Kaleb was his brother goat.

"Wait, Kaleb!" I ran to catch him up, then held his hand so he could splash in the shallow edges of the lake.

I couldn't help but laugh at the look of shock on his face when he touched the cold water. His eyes went wide, but then he laughed his belly laugh and slapped the water with his small hands. Droplets beaded on his hair and glistened in the sun as he bounced and splashed.

I sat down in the shallows and sighed as the cold water floated my tunic up around my stomach. I cupped water on to my burning shoulders with one hand while I held on to Kaleb's sleeve with the other.

I would teach him how to swim when he was older. I'd teach him how to twist and turn and duck and dive. But today he was just going to have to be happy with splashing in the shallow edges.

I picked up a large clatterpod seed and rattled it at him. "Look at this, Kaleb!"

He took the shell off me and used it as a spade, digging into the mud and patting it into small heaps, chatting to himself in his nonsense words.

"You need to learn to speak properly, small brother," I said. "What would Mama say, if she knew you weren't learning your words yet?"

Mama and I used to have long conversations all the time, before Kaleb was born and took up all her energy.

"Stay here, I'm going to check the lake levels." I left Kaleb playing and walked to the edge of the lake.

No wind rippled the calm surface. Midges hummed in the heat and a dragonfly landed on a reed close by. I could see the lake water through its translucent wings.

I licked the sweat salt from my upper lip and looked up to the sky, searching for any sign of rain clouds. Only blue stared back. The great and empty blue.

The lake level measuring stick stuck out of the

water like an arrow in the flank of a beast, and even from paces away, I could see a dark stain, where the lake had sunk even lower. It had gone far below the last whittle mark I'd made the previous dry season.

In the cracked mud, the river reeds were exposed, their roots turning black. I could smell the stink of stagnant water. The shrinking lake left behind puddles where biting insects spawned their eggs and water bugs swam in ever smaller circles.

If the wells and the lake dry up, how will we survive?

From behind me, Tau coughed: the sound he made when something was wrong.

I turned to see him standing next to Kaleb, who was covered in mud, still playing with the clatterpod seed. Tau threw his horns up in the direction of the tall grass.

A bird erupted from the grass with a flurry of feathers, making me jump.

Then I saw it. Distinctive with its mottled black and yellow fur. A large wrathclaw cat.

What's it doing out here? These creatures hunted in the forest canopy and avoided humans at all costs.

Hunger must have driven it out of the forest.

Its oval yellow eyes were trained on Kaleb, who

was oblivious to the creature behind him, still and deadly.

I knew I mustn't run but every sense in my body screamed to get to Kaleb. Without taking my eyes off the cat, I stepped slowly forward.

The wrathclaw cat turned its head and focused on me. I could see it weighing me up, before dismissing me as a threat. It crept forward.

Kaleb waved his arms, chattering at me to play.

Muscles rippled under the cat's tawny coat, sinuous and stealthy. I glimpsed the two protruding canine teeth, long and yellow with age. The paws that could crush a toddling's head.

Mud splattered my bare legs, as Kaleb dug excitedly into the ground. I was close enough to grab him. *Could I outpace a wrathclaw?*

I tried to remember everything Mama had taught me about wildcats, but my mind was blank. I couldn't pull the memory away from the fear, which filled me like smoke.

It was Granny Uma's nagging tone that made it through the fog.

Don't back away from a predator. Make yourself tall. Shout your voice out loud!

I stretched my arms above my head, feeling the

blood drain out of my fingertips. My chest heaved, every rib felt exposed.

One step at a time, I put myself between Kaleb and the cat.

The yellow eyes shifted on to me again, the black pupils blurring out the rest of the world.

The cat whipped its tail, slashing at the grass. It crept closer, the muscles in its shoulders tightened. It was going to attack.

Shout! Granny Uma's voice ordered me.

My tongue stuck to the roof of my mouth. I drew in breath but all that came back out was a wheeze. Tau snorted in warning, still standing over Kaleb.

The wrathclaw cat moved forward. Sand scrunched beneath its heavy paws, leaving claw marks behind.

Be brave. I heard Mama's voice come softly through the fear fog.

My panic-beast tore its way up my throat. It blocked the path of my voice.

I can't. I'm sorry, Mama.

The cat shifted its weight on to its front feet. Its tail swung.

"Maya," Kaleb laughed. He rattled the clatterpod.

The cat's hungry eyes switched back on to my

small brother.

Be brave, Amaya.

I opened my mouth and roared.

Chapter Five

"I won't hurt you"

My chest was on fire. The scream tore from my throat like a living thing, a sound of fear and fury. It filled the world for an eternity in one heartbeat that left me shaking and empty. I sucked a ragged breath back in.

The wrathclaw's eyes widened and its ears flew back flat against its skull. For a moment it stood frozen, then with a spin it fled back into the grass. The only thing left were the deep claw gauges in the sand.

My legs gave way and I crumbled to the ground. A wail filled my ears, but my mouth was shut. I looked down and Kaleb was in tears, screaming. He looked at me like I was a monster.

"It's OK, Kaleb." My words scratched my raw

throat. I tried to pick him up but he squirmed away.

Tau nuzzled his hair and Kaleb clung on to him, still looking at me in alarm.

"I won't hurt you." I tickled his toes, and even though he flinched away I saw a tiny smile. "We need to get home, Kaleb." *The wrathclaw might not have gone far.*

I managed to coax him into a hug. My heart beat fast against his small, shivering body.

The sky was starting to darken. There wasn't much time left – the Switching Hour was coming.

"Tau!" I called out for him to follow. I carried Kaleb back up the path towards the pasture. He was heavy, and my arms soon ached.

Zola and Ela were waiting for us by the pasture gate, their heads swinging in our direction as we came out of the long grass. I put Kaleb down with a groan, but still kept a tight hold of his hand. With the other hand now free, I managed to secure the goats' harnesses.

"Please don't cause a fuss!" I begged them. "Let's just get home." I didn't want to look up at the light draining from the sky; I could *feel* the night approaching over the forest. The cold at my back.

I breathed a sigh of relief when the two goats followed willingly. They kept at my slow pace as I tried to get Kaleb to follow along on his tired feet.

We got home just as the sky overhead began to bruise into purple and red.

I heaved the shed door open and the two goats trotted in. I was glad to see Granny Uma had filled their feed and water pails up that morning. I swung the wooden beam across the door and locked them in for the night.

I cursed under my breath when I heard the chickens clucking from inside the cottage, through the door I'd left open. Their white splatter droppings were all over the floor.

I plopped Kaleb down on the rug while I shooed the chickens outside, slamming the door shut behind them.

Kaleb seemed to have forgotten he had ever been tired. He grabbed my hand and pulled me towards the pantry.

"'ilk!" he screeched.

"You must be hungry," I said. "Let's see what there is to eat." My stomach grumbled at the thought of food.

The food cupboard was organized by Granny

Uma. She liked to be in charge of the meal preparations, so it was a surprise when I opened it and found it almost bare.

"Where's all the food?" There was only one bag of grain, two jars of pickled vegetables, a few strips of meat drying from hooks, as well as a small assortment of fresh vegetables. On the kitchen table there was a chunk of goat's cheese and some bread. Why hadn't Granny Uma told me we were running low on supplies? My mouth went dry, remembering what the fisherman had said.

I'll never let any harm come to Tau, Zola or Ela, I promised myself.

I gathered the fresh vegetables and some millet grain. Thankfully the stove was still warm. I opened the heavy iron door and threw a handful of kindling in. Soon, the stove was hot enough to boil the water.

I used tongs to carry a hot coal to start a fire in the hearth, my hands shaking with the effort of concentration. Granny Uma always made a new kindling stack in the morning, ready for the evening fire, and soon the flames crackled bright.

Before I could chop up the carrots, I heard Kaleb wailing.

Running over to our room, I found him with his head stuck between the cot and the wall.

After easing him loose, I nudged the cot and closed the gap so he wouldn't get trapped again. He triumphantly held up his cotton rag doll.

"MeeMa!" he said. I don't know why he called the doll that. I'd made her from old charcoal sackcloth, with wool hair dyed dark using plant roots. She had a blue dress made from my old shirt and stitched-on pumpkin-seed eyes. Kaleb loved MeeMa.

But Kaleb wasn't distracted by the doll for long. He wrapped himself up in a blanket cocoon, then got tangled and cried for help. I unravelled him, only for him to send the cups on the table clattering.

"'ilk!" His shriek was ear-piercing. I clenched my teeth together.

"I know you're hungry, but you have to wait!" The pot of water began to boil and I added the millet grain. On another hob, I cooked the carrots, pumpkin pieces and cabbage leaves in goat butter.

Kaleb tugged at my clothes and wailed. My head felt like it was splitting into two.

"Here." I unhooked my bracelet. "Play with this."

Two heartbeats later, Kaleb waved the bracelet at me. "Broke!" he shouted.

In dismay, I saw the bracelet had started to unravel where he'd been gnawing on it. I blinked away the first prickle of tears.

"Stop it, Kaleb!" I grabbed the bracelet off him. "I don't know how to look after you, I'm not your mama!"

In Granny Uma's sewing basket, I could only find red wool. It would have to do. I quickly tied the loose ends with the wool and secured the mended bracelet around my wrist.

By now, the whole cottage smelled of overcooked millet and burned vegetables. I sat Kaleb down to eat and placed a plate of food in front of him.

Kaleb wrinkled his nose.

"You said you were hungry." I speared and ate a carrot, ignoring the burnt bitter taste. "Eat it while it's still hot." *It's going to taste a lot worse when it's cold.*

Cajoling a toddling to eat when they don't want to is like trying to stop the rain from falling. It's impossible.

He picked at the millet and ate a mouthful of pumpkin, before deciding it was time to play again. He slid off his chair and chased Tau around the room, knocking over Granny Uma's knitting basket and a stool with her books on top of it.

There was no time to clear up the cooking mess, I had to follow Kaleb around and clear up after him. By the time it was night-dark outside, I'd had enough. "No, Kaleb!" I shouted when he tried to tip the kindling bucket upside down, with MeeMa held tight in his other hand.

He stared at me, and I could see the speckle-glint of mischief in his eyes. Then he grinned and tipped the bucket over.

Kindling and bark dust went all over the rug.

Hot anger burned up all my good sense.

I stomped over. I grabbed MeeMa from his hand and threw her across the room, right into the blazing fire.

The flames licked hungrily at the doll.

Kaleb's eyes went wide, and he opened his baby-toothed mouth and bawled. Louder than his belly laugh, it filled the room with noise. The cottage felt too small for it.

Shock kept me rigid for a heartbeat. Then I grabbed the fire iron and fished the doll out of the flames. Her clothes were charred. Her pumpkin-button eyes burned black.

Kaleb roared. Tears streaked a path through the dried mud on his cheeks.

I scooped him up and pressed my cheek against his hot face. "I'm sorry, Kaleb. I didn't mean to do that." I wiped his tears away with my thumb, my face burning with shame.

I wished Mama was here more than ever.

Kaleb stopped crying once I'd picked him up and soon he was chasing Tau round the room. Once I'd brushed away the doll's singed cloth, I gave her back to Kaleb, who hugged her close.

"I'm sorry I lost my temper, Kaleb." I tickled him and he wriggled away, laughing his belly laugh that made me smile. I loved that sound.

It was close to the midnight moon when I'd finally rocked Kaleb to sleep in my arms, sitting in Granny Uma's chair. I was tired to the insides of my bones. I felt as though I had spent the day herding a thousand goats. I took Mama's stone out of my pocket and held it up. It seemed to glow as the firelight picked out the gold flecks, and I imagined the smile on Mama's face if she could see me now, surrounded by the mess and tired out by looking after my small brother.

You need to be fast to keep up with a toddling, she had told me. *When Kaleb finds his feet, he will leave you behind if you're not careful.*

I tucked the stone back into my pocket and yawned.

Tau slept on the rug amongst the kindling sticks. The leftover millet curdled in the pot. Chicken droppings splattered the earth floor alongside dropped books, balls of wool and blankets.

Granny Uma wasn't going to be happy with the mess, but I was so tired. *I'll get up extra early and clean it up before she gets home. She'll never know!*

I carried Kaleb to his cot and placed him on the mattress. I pulled the cotton blanket over his stomach then squished MeeMa in next to him. Her burned eyes watched me accusingly.

Kaleb's eyes flickered under their lids, and I wondered what he dreamed of. He seemed as innocent as a newborn chick, though the bark dust in his hair and smears of mud told a different story.

Under my breath, I sang the bedtime rhyme.

> *Close your eyes and breathe in deep*
> *It's time for you to go to sleep*
> *Until the moon has gone to hide*
> *I will be right by your side.*

Dragging my feet over to my bed, I curled up under the covers without caring to change out of my clothes. As I drifted off, I had the uneasy feeling of something left undone.

Chapter Six

"What's wrong with you, silly goat?"

The dreams hovered thick on the air, seeping from the cracks and pores of the house. The creature licked its lips.

It snuffled at the underside of the door. The Fire Dreamer was entangled in a nightmare; the creature could taste singed grass and charred bone.

It could smell the dreams of the small boy, the lake water, mud grit and sunburned skin.

Inside, the goat dreamed as well, radiating out the taste of old yams and mash.

Badeko tasted for other sleeping things, but nothing else was there. Its skin prickled, sending a shiver down its arched back.

It reached for the handle and the door cracked open, the firelight glow seeping into the night outside. Extending its head past the door, the creature blinked its milk-white eyes in the brightness. Nothing stirred. The three dreamers were wrapped in sleep.

It followed the scent and snapped at the air with sharp teeth, moving clickety-click on its many legs across the flagstone floor.

It ducked under the stormy nightmare that cloaked the Fire Dreamer, avoiding the lightning crackle and heat that threatened to scorch the creature's skin.

Honey-sweet smells drew it further into the room.

The small boy lay with arms outstretched, his eyes seeing dreams behind their lids.

The creature sang the Song of Sleep, weaving the words into a net, capturing the dream like a shoal of fish. It tightened the net, while the dream strained and fought against the song.

But it was too late. The dream was caught. The boy was trapped.

I woke up with my breath caught in my throat, a stone weighing my body down. *Breathe.* I focused on the rise and fall of my chest. I'd had the nightmare again. I could still see the flames out of the corner of my eye. *It was just a dream.*

Tau bleated and nudged my arm with his horns.

I pushed him away. "It's too early to get up now." I blinked in the half-light.

Tau nipped me. "Ow!" I went to push him away a second time when I noticed he was shaking. "What's wrong with you, silly goat?"

Tau barked his deep warning cough.

"Oh no." I leaped out of bed and ran to Kaleb's cot.

It was empty.

No blanket. No MeeMa.

No Kaleb.

I pressed my hand on the mattress. It was still warm.

"Kaleb!" I spun around. *Maybe he's climbed out by himself?*

The fire was burnt out, but the cottage was flooded with pale morning sun. It took me a heartbeat to find the source of the light.

The open door.

I'm still dreaming. I ran to the door and cupped my hands around my mouth, shouting, "Kaleb!"

I trembled, waiting for a reply.

No Kaleb-sound.

The garden gate was open and Tau stood facing the path that led to the pasture. The same path that led to the lake and—

The forest.

The last slice of the moon disappeared behind the sharp edge of the trees, as the sun rose up in the east.

The Switching Hour had passed.

With a jolt, I remembered the sound of a baby's cry, the night before. The humming song that had seeped under the door.

Badeko.

It couldn't be.

"Kaleb!" I ran towards the garden, where he loved to play amongst the cabbage leaves.

I hunted through the cabbage patch and the dusty holes from where yams had long since been plucked. I called his name, over and over until my voice croaked.

I checked the cottage. I opened up cupboards. I even pulled apart the cot, to see if he'd got stuck underneath.

The room was empty of anyone else but me.

I ran outside, into the sun. I shut my eyes tight, but all I could hear was the sound of the baby crying. The song that had seeped through the cracks in the door.

Badeko.

It's taken my small brother.

I bent over as if I'd been stomach-punched. I clutched my sides and howled at the ground. Tears wet my toes and made mud spots in the dirt.

My heart pounded in my ears and my vision blurred. A tingling spread across my hands as I shook uncontrollably.

Kaleb. His name hammered against my throat but I couldn't speak. I couldn't think.

I was dimly aware of Tau pressing his forehead against my shoulder. Nothing else felt real.

Dizziness swept over me, I couldn't get enough air into my lungs, I was breathing too fast. My lungs felt too small.

"What have I done?" The words hissed through my clenched teeth.

He's gone. Kaleb is gone.

The panic-beast clawed at my insides.

What am I going to do?

I fumbled for the stone in my pocket. I grasped it and squeezed it tight, until my nails dug into my palm.

"What do I do, Mama?" I cried out. The shame and guilt flooded over my whole body like freezing water, making me tremble violently. *How could I have failed to look after him? It's all my fault.*

"I'm so sorry, Mama!" I sobbed into my hands, pressing the stone against my cheek. "I don't know what to do!"

But even though she was gone, I knew what she would say. *Find him, Amaya. Bring him home.*

Chapter Seven

"I'll come back to you"

I have to find Kaleb. I took a long, slow breath. *I have to pull myself together.*

Forcing myself to stand up, I viciously scrubbed the tears from my eyes.

Think, Amaya! Feeling lost, I stared at the path that led away from the cottage, towards Town. I desperately wanted Granny Uma to appear, even though I knew she'd be more than furious with me. I needed her to fix it. To make everything OK again.

How could I have been so stupid to think I could have looked after Kaleb by myself?

"But what if it's too late to wait for Granny Uma?" I whispered out loud.

I gripped hold of Tau's collar, feeling like he was the only thing anchoring me to the earth.

The sun was tall in the sky, but soon it would begin to stoop towards the earth.

I needed to find Kaleb *now*.

I ran to the start of the path, searching for signs of Granny Uma. The heat haze blurred the far end of the track, but there was no one making their way towards the cottage. No shadow on the horizon. If the baby struggled to be born, Granny Uma might not even come back today.

If this is truly the work of Badeko – and what else could it be? – how long until I begin to forget Kaleb? Will I catch the Sorrow Sickness before I can get to him? Panic rose within me like a column of choking smoke.

I can't wait for Granny Uma.

I must be brave, like Mama.

It didn't take me long to gather my things into a pack.

A change of clothes. A length of rope that I tied around my waist. From the shelf above my bed, I found my tinderbox. Made of copper, it had *Amaya* stamped into the surface of the lid. It had been a gift from Mama. My shaking fingers rattled the flint and tinder inside, but I didn't open it. I hadn't touched it since the fire that took Mama away from me. I shoved it to the bottom of my bag.

From the kitchen, I grabbed the bag of grain, a jar of pickled vegetables, goat's cheese and two loaves of bread that I wrapped in a cloth, and a skin pouch of water. Lastly, I rummaged through Granny Uma's medicine bookshelf.

"Granny Uma said Badeko's nest is in the forest," I told Tau, who was snuffling at my pack. "I need to find someone who knows the way to the Dead Tree and can help me find Kaleb."

Tau trotted over as I flipped open a notebook, curious to see what I'd found.

The notebook was filled with Granny Uma's drawings of the plants and flowers she'd found while foraging. Stembark plants, with their ability to numb pain. Yellow prickle-peach flowers, that drew out infections. Coffee beans for antioxidant remedies. Each specimen meticulously drawn in charcoal pencil.

Flicking to the front of the notebook, I was relieved to find a map showing the trail to the Forest Settlement.

"I can use this to find a woodcutter," I said to Tau, whose yam-mash-scented breath fluttered the pages.

I found a lump of charcoal in the hearth and used it to write a note to Granny Uma on a page ripped from the notebook.

Kaleb is missing. I'm going to the Forest Settlement to find help. I need to find Badeko and bring Kaleb back home, I scrawled.

Seeing the words written down made the guilt burn all over again. I pictured Granny Uma's face when she found out that Kaleb had been taken and it was all my fault. She had seemed to age so much since Mama had gone, her eyes tired and her hair greyer. I couldn't imagine what this would do to her.

I stifled a sob. Crying wasn't going to help.

I need to make it right.

Leaving the note on the table, amongst the leftover vegetable peels and dirty bowls, I studied the charcoal piece in my hand.

It was the same dark black as Kaleb's eyes. I tucked it into my pocket, nestling it next to the stone the colour of Mama's eyes. It would help me remember.

I wriggled the pack on to my shoulders. I made sure my axe was secured to my belt by lightly touching the silver tip with my finger. The sharp sting of metal was reassuring.

On Granny Uma's chair lay her neatly folded shawl. Age hadn't softened the colours: stripes and patterns in red, orange and yellow that could blur your eyes if you stared long enough.

I carefully packed it into the bag. Kaleb might need something familiar and warm to wear when I found him.

I let the chickens out of the coop and Ela and Zola out of the shed. I didn't have time to take them to the field; they would have to be content to stay in the garden. Granny Uma would shut them away when she was back from the Eastern Town.

The sun was gaining strength. *I have to hurry*, I thought. *But first I have to say goodbye.*

I squeezed my eyes tight, but I couldn't put it off any longer.

Tau waited by the garden gate. He bleated when he saw me, stamping the dirt with his hoof. I wrapped my arms around his neck, and he pushed his broad forehead against my shoulder.

"You can't come with me, Tau. I can't put your life in danger," I whispered in his twitching ear. "Granny Uma will be back soon. She'll look after you."

I kissed his nose, breathing in the smell of wool and straw and dung that Granny Uma complained about in the cottage. But Tau smelled more like home than a house ever could.

I closed the garden gate behind me and latched it shut. Tau would have free roam of the garden, and the goat shed. There was hay for him to eat and water in the trough.

But it felt like I was leaving behind my courage. Tau, my companion. My goat-shaped shadow.

I clenched my jaw and walked away. The fence rattled as Tau headbutted the closed gate, and he bleated in surprise.

"I'm sorry, Tau! I'll come back to you," I called out, without turning around.

I kept my eyes on the tear-blurred path in front of me. I turned the corner that hid the cottage behind the thicket of needle-thorn trees, yet still I could hear Tau's cries.

But I knew that a dark and strange forest was no place for a goat. Kaleb being snatched away was my fault, and I alone needed to fix it.

The trees stretched towards the sky, taller than me ten times over, their branches bent over the path that had been hacked through the thicket. I took a deep breath and followed the trail, leaving the bright sunshine of the grasslands behind. I shivered as the shade sucked the heat out of the air.

Dead leaves swished and swirled around my legs as I walked. I had never seen the trees as bare as this before. The drought had stripped them clean.

Soon, I'd lost the edge of the grasslands in the twists and turns of the trail. The canopy sealed away the sky and the forest became my whole world.

The pale light that filtered down through the branches made my courage feel small. I was used to wide open space, the grassland and the lake, where I could read the sun as it travelled across the sky. I wasn't used to being hemmed in on both sides by trees.

I started running, hearing the *swish* of my feet through the leaves. I repeated the name of my small brother as I ran, a song that lengthened my strides and propelled me *faster, faster, faster.*

I kept running until a seam of fire licked down my sides, and I had to stop. Hunched over, I winced at the pain in my chest. I gulped down air as hot as steam that dried my mouth to dust. I unhooked my pouch and swallowed down small sips of tepid water, careful not to drink too much. I tied up the leather strings tight around the pouch and looked upwards, searching for rain clouds through the branches, but the tiny slivers of sky were clear and blue.

Maybe I can get a better look up there, to see how far I've come?

I avoided the sharp needle-thorn trees, instead picking a densewood tree with low-hanging branches and cracked bark that proved easy to cling on to. Some of the branches were brittle from the drought, so I carefully tested each one before I put my full weight on it. I climbed as high as I dared, and clung on to the main trunk with one hand, moving the topmost branch out of the way to get a view.

I hissed through my teeth. The forest was a dark sea of skeleton trees, going on as far as the horizon on all sides. I tried to peer back towards the cottage, but I couldn't see the grasslands or the lake. I felt smaller than a termite.

How much time do I have left?

I shaded my eyes and squinted upwards, only to find that the sun had fallen three-quarters of the way down towards the west. I had less daylight remaining than I'd thought.

I scrambled back down so fast my knees were scoured open, while shards of bark made blood blossom under my fingernails. I sucked out the splinters and spat them on the ground. My spit disappeared into the thirsty earth in the time it took to blink.

Studying the map, I could see the red cross that indicated the Forest Settlement. I could make it there before the Switching Hour if I was fast.

"Hey!" The voice made me jump.

At first, I couldn't see where it had come from, then I spotted two faces peering out of a hole in the ground, in a small clearing away from the path. A woman and a boy child.

"Over here!" The woman waved me over.

Hesitating for a moment, I stepped off the path and walked over to them.

"What are you doing?" I asked the woman. Dust coated her hair and skin. There was a shovel in her hand and the child, younger than me, but older than Kaleb, carried a bucket. He held it up triumphantly for me to see.

I peered inside.

Three fat speckled toads, already dead.

"We're digging for toads; we'll roast them for supper." He grinned. The woman heaved herself out of the deep hole with an effort then reached to take the bucket from the boy.

She held it out to me. "Would you like one, to take to your family?"

The dead-eyed toads stared up at me. "I've never eaten a toad," I said, shaking my head.

"You can't turn your nose up at food in a drought," she snapped. "You have to be resourceful."

I realized that it must have taken her most of the day to dig that hole.

"What are you doing out here alone?" the woman asked. "We're heading back to the Eastern Town, before it starts to get dark. You should come with us."

I shook my head. "I'm going to the Forest Settlement."

The woman frowned. "There's no one left there, except..." She hesitated, taking hold of the boy's hand. "It'll be safer if you head back to the Town. There's nothing left in the forest but sorrow. Don't you know Badeko is back? You'll be in great danger once the Switching Hour has come."

"I'm looking for someone."

The woman's pity didn't need words. I could feel it in waves.

She turned back towards the path, in the direction I'd come from. The boy watched me over his shoulder, until they were hidden from view by the tall grass.

I hope they make it back to Town before the Switching Hour.

I turned back to the trail and ran as if a wild dog snapped at my heels.

Even without reading the sun, I could feel the Switching Hour draw near. My eyes widened as I tried to follow the path and avoid stumbling into burrow holes in the lessening light. There was no sign of the dust-hogs that had made the dens.

All around me were the shrieking calls of the weaving birds as they flew back to their tunnel-shaped nests in the needle-thorn trees. I caught the flash of their yellow feathers in the shadows.

The sky softened into pink and gold, and the birdsong began to quieten down.

I ran on, my heart pounding in my chest.

The Switching Hour had begun.

The path wound through the bare trees, deeper and deeper into the forest.

Once the sun set, the darkness fell like a stone.

Then my ears pricked up at a new sound. At first, I thought it was the cricket hum from the long grass. But this was different. I stopped and listened, pushing my hair away from my ears. I heard a *tic-tic-tic* clicking. Looking up at the canopy, my heartbeat stuttered.

Milk-white eyes stared back at me.

Chapter Eight

"This can't be real!"

Spinning on my heel, I sprinted away, faster than I'd ever run before. The wind whistled past my ears. The ground was air beneath my feet.

On either side, the forest was a grey blur. I could just make out the path, but all the colour and depth had left with the sun.

A skittering in the branches caught the corner of my eye. *Keep running!*

Pain stabbed my shoulder, making me cry out. I grasped at it and felt a small body squeezed under my fingers. Fur and leathery wings. Clawed wing tips hooked deep into my skin.

I slowed to a halt. *A bat!*

To my surprise, it squeaked and vanished and I was left holding empty air.

I spun around looking for it, when sharp teeth knifed my arm, making me yelp. Another bat had secured itself, with claws that hooked and dug into my skin.

My fingers fumbled. I managed to tear it from my arm as another bat flew into my hair and tangled itself up in the curls. Its teeth sank into my scalp and scraped against skull-bone. I screamed at the lightning-hot pain, even as the bat I'd captured disappeared from my grasp like smoke.

"This *can't* be real!" I tore at another bat, yanking out chunks of my hair with it.

The moon was hidden behind the trees. I'd lost the path.

Panic seeped into my blood like poison.

A *swish* and *swoop* past my ear. Then another stab of pain.

I clawed at my neck where a bat had sunk its teeth in. I snatched away the leather wings, but more and more took its place.

I grappled with the flapping, squeaking creatures. My stomach flipped as the warm bodies squeezed under my fingers, but their teeth wouldn't release their grip. They clamped on as tight as a burr-seed.

I stumbled, falling with a thump that *whooshed*

the air from my lungs, my head hitting the ground with a crack against stone. The bolt of pain took my breath away. A trickle of wetness slipped down the side of my face.

I curled up and tried to protect my neck, but the bats swarmed. Their quick claws latched on as they crawled like mice across my clothes, looking for exposed skin.

This isn't real, I told myself, even as spikes of pain contracted my muscles tight.

I wasn't aware of the song until it seeped into my head. A humming that reverberated against my skull. The pain vanished, as if the song was balm. The song wrapped itself around me like a bandage secured too tight.

Even without words, I knew the melody. I'd heard it the night that our cottage had been surrounded by the sound of a baby crying.

Badeko's song.

From my pocket, I fumbled Mama's stone into the palm of my hand and squeezed it with both hands.

"Mama!" I shouted with all my breath.

A bleating call echoed my howl. I strained against the humming that had filled every space in my head. I fought the buzzing blackness that fizzed at the edges of my sight, as panic tightened the knots in my stomach.

Then I heard it again. The bark of a goat.

"Tau!" I screamed his name as loud as I could.

There he was, tearing a track through the long grass, his white coat shining like a beacon in the darkness.

Tau! I should have known the clever goat would have found a way to escape.

"I'm here!" I gasped, almost weeping with relief. He slipped to a halt beside me and I clambered on to his broad back, wrapping my hands around his neck.

"Run, Tau!" I shouted, and he set off at full speed.

Chapter Nine

"We need to get inside!"

I shook the threads of the song from my head, as Tau leaped back on to the path and carried me away like a rocket. I blinked away the blackness and breathed out the roiling feeling in the pit of my stomach.

As the wind whistled past my ears and the blood from the wound on my head dried stiff, I knew we were still in danger.

Through the dark Tau ran, keeping to the path. He leaped over tree roots and dodged burrow holes. Agile and fast, he tore through the shadow-forest without a trip or a slip.

All around us, I heard the shriek of the wood-toads. They'd come out of their burrows to look for insects, millipedes and scuttling beetles.

Rustling sounds from the dead leaves made

me shiver. I'd heard stories of giant forest snakes and I imagined them winding through the trees, searching for a goat and a girl to eat. I longed for the safety of Granny Uma's cottage, that we'd left far behind. A nightjar's churring call sounded close by, then I felt its wings vibrating the air as it flew past us.

Every sound was heard against the backdrop of the cricket noise that swelled and undulated, leaving no space of silence. It was maddening when you were trying to listen out for danger and jumping at every sound.

How far until we get to the Forest Settlement? The branches hid the moon, I couldn't make out how much time we'd spent outside after the Switching Hour. I felt the tug of fear in my belly. *Badeko must be nearby.*

Hadn't Granny Uma told me before, "No one is safe from Badeko the Dream Eater at night, no matter how fast you think you can run"?

Suddenly, the path opened up into a moonlit clearing.

Cart tracks were furrowed into the dirt and empty market stalls stood in rows, some with bunting trailing loose. Wooden boxes lay abandoned.

Tau slowed down and I jumped off his back,

swaying as I landed. My head throbbed from where I'd hit it on the ground earlier, which now seemed like a lifetime ago.

"Hello?" I called out, but no one answered back.

Branching off from the clearing were paved paths leading to cottages. They all looked like Granny Uma's home with thatch roofs and clay-brick walls.

Nothing moved. No chickens clucked from the hen houses, no animals stamped and snorted from the paddocks. Even the cricket noise was barely a whisper here.

Tau coughed a warning and backtracked until he bumped against an empty chicken carrier. His hoof caught on the wires and he leaped into the air, rattling the cage.

"Calm, Tau!" I released him with trembling fingers.

I hugged him close, both our heartbeats banging like drums. Tau snorted and shook his horns. He shivered against my chest.

"We need to get inside!" I cried.

Running up to the first cottage, I hammered on the door.

"Let me in, please let me inside!"

I leaned against the door. I was sure I could hear

something, whispers muffled by the wood. The hush of held breath.

"Please!" I banged on the door again, kicking it with my heel.

It creaked open.

I pulled Tau inside and closed the door behind me.

The cottage was small and dark, with only a candle flickering on the wooden table. No fire burned in the hearth.

"Hello?" I whispered. My skin prickled with the sense that something wasn't right.

Two pairs of eyes stared back at me.

A man and a woman sat by the table. It was difficult to make them out at first as they were wrapped up in black blankets, merging with the shadows in the room.

The woman stood up. She clasped her hands tightly, knotting her fingers together.

"Thank you, you saved us!" I said to her, feeling the relief at being inside and safe from Badeko. "I'm so glad there's someone still here. I thought everyone had moved to the Town."

The woman smiled wide and stretched out her arms to wrap me in a hug, but I instinctively ducked away. Something flashed too brightly in her eyes. *Panic? Fear?*

I gripped on to Tau's collar.

"Our child!" The woman said the words in a hiccup, like they'd had been in her throat for too long. "You're back!"

"I'm not your child." The uneasiness in the pit of my stomach grew. Now that I was inside, I could smell the sorrow. The air was heavy, stale with it.

"Come, sit down with us." The woman grabbed my arm, determined not to let me go. "We've kept your place, ready for your return." She dragged me over to the table as I clung on to Tau's collar.

"You're hurting me!" I said, trying to pull away, but she wasn't listening. The man just watched as I was dragged over to the vacant chair at the head of the table.

Something told me if I sat down, I wouldn't be able to leave. As if sitting down at the empty place would be confirmation that I *was* theirs. Like I belonged here.

My mouth went dry. "Let me go!" I strained against her, feeling the pinch in my arm as her grip cut off the circulation. "I'm not your child, I'm Amaya!"

"Sit down!" The sudden flash of anger in her voice

made me lose my stance. I stumbled forward, letting go of Tau's collar. I knocked into the chair, sending it crashing to the ground.

The man jumped up, righting the chair in a swift movement.

"Clumsy!" His voice was deep and rumbly. Taking no notice as I struggled against the woman's grip, he laughed heartily. "We're just so happy to have you back."

Tau shifted next to me, anxiously trotting back and forth.

"I'm not sitting in that chair."

"Of course you are! It's where you always sit." The woman reached out with both hands to smooth my hair away from my face, letting go of my arm in the process. Her eyes didn't register when I flinched away from her touch.

"We've missed you so much," she murmured. "Come and sit with us."

I backed slowly away as confusion swept over the faces of the couple.

"Come on, Tau," I whispered. "We're leaving."

"Where are you going?" the woman said. She reached out with her twisted fingers, snatching at the air between us.

I turned and ran towards the door, opening it and leaping over the porch, my hand still on Tau's collar, dragging him with me.

I looked over my shoulder and saw the woman standing silently in the open doorway. As if seeing the outside for the first time, she clutched on to the doorframe, staring towards the forest like a small child frightened of the dark.

I followed her gaze. The forest was an impenetrable gloom. Suddenly, a branch on a densewood tree bent under the weight of something I couldn't see. Tau snorted, his eyes rolling in fear. My heartbeat hammered in my throat.

The woman shuffled back into the house, slamming the door behind her. Even as afraid as I was, there was no way I was going back there.

There must be somewhere else to hide!

My eye snagged on a glint in the dark. A light in the window of a cottage, tucked behind a gnarled marago tree. Smoke poured from the chimney.

"But what if there's people acting strangely in there as well?" I hissed at Tau, as if he knew the answer. I looked back towards the forest.

The branch creaked again. Something thumped to the ground. Something big and heavy.

A wrathclaw? A giant snake? Badeko?

"Run, Tau!" We hurtled towards the cottage and cleared its porch in a bound. I pounded against the door and shouted, "Let us in!"

Chapter Ten

"What are you?"

"Let me in!" Desperation cracked my voice into a million pieces. I hammered on the door with my fists.

"What are you?" came a muffled voice.

"Please, let me in!" I shouted through the cracks in the wood. I pressed my ear against the door and listened.

"How do I know you're not the Dream Eater?" the voice replied, low and urgent.

"Please," I shouted. "If you don't let me in, Badeko will get me and it'll be all your fault!" Anger boiled up inside me and I pounded my fist on the door, kicking it with my foot.

The door cracked open, and I fell inside, Tau leaping in after me. The door slammed shut and the lock swung into place.

I lay on my back and pulled air into my aching lungs.

A red-haired girl stared down at me, an axe raised in one hand.

"What's your name?" she demanded.

"Amaya." I scrambled to my feet and backed away, pulling Tau with me.

"Why are you outside after the Switching Hour?" The girl glared at me and raised the axe higher.

"I'm looking for my brother." I held up my hands. "Please put the axe down, I'm no threat."

The girl stuck her chin out. "Do you have any weapons on you?"

"I've got my own axe." With my hands still raised, I moved sideways on, showing her the axe attached to my belt. "You can take it off me, if you like."

The girl unhooked it from my belt, still holding hers upwards. She weighed it in her hand appreciatively.

"Where did you get this from?"

"It was my mama's axe." I was really proud of it. The axe head was steel with a patterned handle made from densewood. I could still make out the carved needle-thorn flowers, though they had become faded and worn by her hands and mine.

"It's a good axe." The girl handed it back to me.

I attached it back on to my belt with trembling fingers. Slowly my breathing calmed.

"I'm Mally," the girl said, leaning her axe against the wall by the door. Her voice was deep and she spoke her words as if she didn't want to let them go. She looked about my age, maybe a little older.

Tau nudged my hand and I wrapped my arms around his neck, hugging him close, whispering *Thank you, thank you for coming to find me.*

Mally examined me. "You're covered in blood. What happened?"

"I hit my head." I tried to rub the blood off, wincing at the cut that had swollen up as big as a stone. "I was running from *something*. I thought it was a swarm of bats but they disappeared when Tau arrived, as if they had been an illusion…" I trailed off, not knowing how to explain it to her.

"Badeko can make you see and feel things that aren't real," Mally said, watching me carefully. I couldn't read her expression, but the intensity of it chilled me. Then she clucked her tongue.

"Let me put some ointment on the wound. I have some aloe leaves. I can make a poultice."

I watched her rummage through the cupboards,

pulling out bundles of herbs and dried flowers and placing them on the table. She sniffed the leaves before she crushed them with a wooden mortar and pestle.

Tau seemed to forget his fears. He nuzzled my pack, looking for food. I rubbed the spot behind his ears and leaned my head against his neck, smelling the straw and dust that clung to him like a cloak. "I promise to give you a big bowl of yam mash when we get home."

Mally came and kneeled down next to us.

"Here," she said, handing me a wooden bowl with a green paste inside.

I cautiously patted it on to the lump on my forehead then let out a sigh as the cold paste soothed away the pain.

"Thank you." I smiled at her. "If it wasn't for you, we'd still be out there." I shivered at the thought of the woman and the man from earlier. "I tried to get help from another cottage. There were two people inside and they thought I was their child!"

The girl nodded. "They think everyone's their missing child."

"What do you mean?"

"Badeko took Sara and Peter's child a few weeks

ago. Since then, Sara has grown more and more confused, trying to claim other people's children as her own."

"And Peter?"

"He stays indoors. I sometimes hear him laughing, talking to Sara as though their child is still in the house with them." The girl shuddered. "It's really creepy."

"It's really sad." My heart ached for them, now the fright had worn off. *It's so cruel, what Badeko has done to them.*

"People have been taking them food and the other villagers tried to persuade them to move to the Town, but they won't leave. They're convinced their missing child will turn up."

"What about you, do you think the missing children will be found?"

Mally paused, eyes downcast. "No. I think Badeko has taken them away for ever."

The panic-beast flared in my chest. *Kaleb.*

"I haven't seen you around here before." Mally tilted her head and narrowed her eyes. "Where've you come from?" There was still a wariness in her voice.

"From the grassland, near the sunken lake."

"Is this your goat?" Mally reached out and stroked Tau's neck. To my surprise, he rubbed his head against her hand. He was usually nervous with people he didn't know. She laughed when he tried to nibble her fingers.

"He's mine. I raised him," I said, more snappily than I meant. In a softer tone, I added, "His name's Tau."

"Hello, Tau," she said. She scratched under his chin, and he closed his eyes with a look of bliss on his face. I tweaked his tail then glanced around the room. It was like our cottage: logs piled neatly against the wall closest to the hearth, heavy roof beams painted white and windows in the thick stone walls.

"Are your parents here?" I asked, looking back at Mally. Her eyes were bright green. I'd never seen eyes like hers before. Granny Uma's and Mama's eyes were deep brown, and Kaleb's and mine were black.

Mally continued to stroke Tau. She shook her head.

"Where are they?"

"They're taking a supply of wood to the Eastern Town. They'll be gone a few days."

"I don't have a few days to wait! My brother has been taken by Badeko." Tears prickled. "I must get to the Dead Tree before it's too late and I forget he exists!"

"Is that why you're alone in the forest after the Switching Hour?" Mally asked.

"I'd been looking after him on my own all day. I was so tired, I forgot to lock the door last night. He was gone by the morning." The words stuck in my throat. It still didn't feel real. A tiny spark inside me hoped I would wake up and hear Kaleb call my name from his cot.

Mally looked grim. "The Dream Eater has already taken five from the Forest Settlement and five more from the Eastern Town."

"The night before last I heard Badeko's song, from under the door."

"It could have been a nightmare."

I shook my head. "My nightmares are different." I placed my hand over my pocket, feeling the heavy outline of the stone inside. I felt the sudden flare and heat of flames. *Mama.*

A daggertooth jackal howled, a faraway sound that still made me jump. All I could think about was that Kaleb was out there, somewhere.

Please be safe! I had to fight the urge to run outside into the darkness and search every tree and every burrow hole until I found him. *I have three sunrises before his dreams get eaten up and he's lost to me for ever.* Remembering the charcoal in my pocket, I carefully took it out and held it in my palm. The wood was fragile and bits of black dust rubbed off on my fingers.

I thought of Kaleb covered in mud next to the lake. Kaleb, as he gnawed on pumpkin rind under the table. His toothy smile. His dark eyes, just like mine. *I can still remember him.* I tucked the charcoal back into my pocket, next to Mama's stone.

"It looks like you're staying here for the night then. You and your goat." Mally nodded at the hearth. "I have soup, still in the pot. I'll stoke up the stove."

She gathered kindling from the woven basket next to the hearth and rolled a log from the woodpile with her feet. It rumbled over the flagstone floor.

There was a wooden table with an elaborately carved surface in the centre of the room. I ran my hands over the top of it, tracing the outlines that were polished smooth.

I'd never seen anything like it. "This is beautiful."

Mally glanced up from feeding the fire. "Papa made it. He carves furniture to sell in the towns, as well as firewood."

The carvings had been designed in two parts. On one side, there was a round sun with slices of light radiating outwards. I recognized densewood trees with their cracked bark and needle-thorn trees, complete with weaving birds building cocoon nests in the branches. I spotted sheep, cows and goats. Lush crops of wheat and corn were whittled into the wood, underneath clouds of rain.

I brushed my fingers along the other side of the table. I traced the full moon, with its pitted face. The trees were gnarled and bare of leaves, the fields empty of their crops. There were deep carvings of shadow shapes with eyes, slitted pupils that followed me as I moved around the table. A shiver tracked its way down my back.

Day and night. The rains and drought.

Moving away from the table, I studied the rest of the room.

A woven reed chair had been placed near the hearth, with a woollen blanket folded on the seat. Two beds were up against the wall on opposite sides of the room, along with a crib that looked just like

Kaleb's. There were paintings on the walls, of the forest and people and animals.

The space certainly wasn't as neat and tidy as Granny Uma's cottage. It felt like the home we'd shared with Mama: colourful, messy and warm.

I went over and sat down next to Mally as she fed kindling through the open stove door. Tau curled up in front of the fire. He tucked his head against his side, his curved horns nestled in his fur. I was glad he was here, but I worried for his safety. I needed to be strong to fight Badeko. *Maybe Mally would allow Tau to stay with her until I came back?* I glanced at her. Her forehead was wrinkled in thought; her eyes narrowed as she watched the flames build.

"Is your well still bringing in water?" I asked.

Mally nodded. "It's low, but the water is there. For now," she said. She tried to hide her worry with a shrug, but I could see it in the downturn of her mouth.

The soup had begun to bubble in the pot. The room filled with the smell of spicy groundfruit, and my nose tingled with a whiff of pepper. Mally brought bowls over, and she ladled out two portions.

Tau uncurled himself and snuffled in the direction of the bowls. "Not for you, Tau," I laughed.

"I have something for him," Mally said. She brought over two large cabbage leaves from the kitchen.

"Thank you," I said, wishing I could give her something in return. I remembered the jar of pickled vegetables in my pack. I took it out and opened it, setting it down on the table next to the bowls for soup.

I held each rubbery leaf out to the goat, feeling the tug as Tau chomped and crunched, his beard swinging.

Mally passed me a bowl of soup. The steam rose against my cheek and my mouth watered. I could see her staring at me intently as I began to eat.

I wonder if Kaleb is hungry? Or whether he feels anything while he is in Badeko's deep sleep? The thought made the food lose its flavour.

When we'd both finished the soup and the pickled vegetables, Mally took the empty bowls and went over to the kitchen area. A white-tailed hare hung from a hook on the ceiling, as well as a bream strung up to dry, its silver scales shimmering in the lamplight.

Something was troubling me. "Why did your parents leave you all alone? Couldn't you have gone with them?"

Mally wiped her hands on her green dress. "I stayed to look after the chickens," she said quietly.

I could hear the lie in her words. Her voice trembled under the weight of the untruth.

"Are you not worried about Badeko?"

"I can look after myself," Mally snapped. "Besides, I love this house; it's where I've always lived. I didn't want to leave."

"I'm sorry, I didn't mean anything by it," I said. I knew that something wasn't right with her story but I didn't want to annoy her further.

I wrapped an arm around Tau's belly and leaned my head against his side, hearing the *thump-thump-thump* of his heartbeat. I yawned and closed my eyes. It felt like for ever since I'd slept.

Mally nudged me with her foot. "You can sleep in the other bed. It will be better than the floor and a goat for a pillow."

"Thank you," I mumbled. I fell into the bed with an exhausted sigh. I could hardly muster the energy to pull the blankets over my aching body.

As my eyelids began to close, Mally snuggled under the blankets in the other bed, wrapping herself up in a cocoon, her long hair spilling out from the folds.

Tau jumped on to the end of my bed, his hooves digging into the straw mattress. He shuffled around until he found a comfortable position, almost tipping me out of bed in the process.

With Mally's heavy breathing assuring me she was asleep, I whispered the bedtime rhyme, wishing there was some way that Kaleb would hear it.

> *Close your eyes and breathe in deep*
> *It's time for you to go to sleep*
> *Until the moon has gone to hide*
> *I will be right by your side.*

I fought sleep for as long as I could, dreading the nightmares that would surely come. But you can't stay awake for ever.

The boy slept in the hollow. Quiet breath. Closed eyes. The creature had a stomach full of dreams, and more fought against the net that trapped the boy. Dreams that smelled of needle-thorn leaves and sun-baked earth. Dreams that tasted of pumpkin and porridge. The child dreamed of the girl. The Fire Dreamer. The creature could sense the bone-deep connection between her and the boy.

It hoped the boy would bring her to it. But not yet. It was still too weak.

The creature turned its milk-white eyes towards the starry sky. No clouds scarred the bright moon tonight. It contemplated the lasting drought. Without the rains, the creature was stuck, halfway between this world and the next. It was born by the drought and passed away with the rains. Death and rebirth. Over and over again.

When the creature had first awoken, it had started small, dining on the dreams of the birds, that smelled of sky and song, then the crocodiles, who dreamed of fish and flesh. As the drought progressed, the creature had turned to the dreams of children to satisfy its increasing hunger.

But the drought was holding tight and the creature's hunger grew bigger still. It needed more than a child's dreams could provide. And with each feed, the creature grew stronger. Strong enough to ensnare a nightmare.

Once it had feasted on a nightmare, one as fierce as the girl's, it would be strong enough to capture all dreamers.

It would even be strong enough to capture the Old Ones, those fully-grown children. Their dreams were strange and muddled up, and harder to capture. They swirled with all the remembering, layer upon layer of memories, all fighting to be relived. Sweet one moment and sour the next, the stench of fear and the fragrance of wishful thoughts.

The creature could smell it all and it wanted to devour it all.

It scuttled out of the hollow, its legs catching hold of the cracks in the bark. Once on the ground, it sniffed the air, before heading back into the forest.

Chapter Eleven

"The ancient Bao Tree"

I shuddered awake.

The dream was still wrapped tightly around my head, and my hair was damp with sweat. I gasped for air, instinctively listening for Kaleb's quiet breathing, before I remembered he was gone.

I'd been dreaming of before, when we'd lived together, just Mama and me, before Kaleb had been born. Mama had taught me everything, how to swim, fish and cook. Then I'd made friends and wanted to play with them, not be my mama's shadow. Last night I'd dreamed of the kisses she planted on my head as I wriggled to be free of her embrace. The goodbyes I'd thrown over my shoulder, not realizing there would be a final one.

Then, as always, the dream had turned into flames. The crackle and pop of burning wood.

I'd seen a tree, white as bones. It looked upside down, with roots reaching towards the sky. The Dead Tree.

Is that where Kaleb's been taken?

I groaned and opened my eyes. Slowly my vision adjusted to the dark of the room. I breathed in, expecting to smell smoke.

"It was just a dream," I whispered, even as I imagined I could taste charcoal on my tongue. Straw and red clay burned up.

Pale pink and golden shafts of dawn light streamed in through the cracks in the shuttered windows. I rubbed away the sleep crust from my eyes.

For a moment I thought I'd overslept, but the noise of the early birds reassured me that the sun was only just starting to rise.

Tau was already awake and sniffing at the underside of the cottage door.

Mally's bed was empty, her blanket tossed in a heap on the floor.

I rolled out of bed, smoothing out the creases in my tunic.

Tau bounded out as soon as I opened the door. He twisted up in the air and bucked his legs in joy at being outside.

I grinned. "Silly goat."

The cottage was built in a well-kept clearing. Trees were sparse enough for grass to grow, although the drought had turned the blades brittle-yellow.

Under the marago tree, a rusty chicken cage lay empty and broken. *Why had Mally lied about staying to look after the chickens?*

I heard the slosh of water and peered around the side of the cottage.

A well had been built nearby, its stone walls knee-high. Mally was pulling on the rope – hand over hand she heaved, until the bucket came into sight. She pulled it over the wall, water slopping over the sides of it. She peered into the bucket and frowned, before she poured the water, which was clouded with red silt, into a wooden pail by her side.

"Hi, Mally." I walked over, Tau trotting beside me.

She nodded hello, then motioned to the bucket. "You can wash with this water, but I'm going to have to boil some more for drinking." She sighed. "It used to be clear. Now the bucket is scraping the bottom of the well."

I let Tau have a quick drink, before I nudged him out the way and plunged my hands into the water, while Mally drew more out of the well. I used the damp hem of my tunic to dab at the wound on my head.

"Do you know where I'd find a white tree?" I asked Mally. "It looks upside down, with branches like roots?" I didn't really expect her to know what I was talking about.

But Mally nodded. "The ancient Bao Tree."

My heart beat faster.

"It's two days' walk from here," she said. "Why do you want to know?"

"Granny Uma said Badeko lives in a nest under the Dead Tree. That's where Kaleb will be." It was my only hope. "Maybe it's the same one."

Mally stared at me, her eyes narrowed. "It could be," she said. "The tree has been around for as long as anyone can remember."

She glanced upwards. "I'll start boiling the water. It should be done by the time the sun is up." She walked back to the cottage, the water slopping on to the same green dress she'd been wearing the night before.

I followed Mally into the house. Tau was already

inside, snuffling around my pack for food. I shooed him away and pulled the pack on to my shoulders, distributing the weight of it to make it more comfortable.

Mally had set the boiled water to cool on the stone floor, next to water pouches waiting to be filled.

"Thank you for your help," I said. Even though I knew that time was precious, my stomach squirmed with the thought of walking through the forest by myself.

Tau bumped my hand with his nose. My throat constricted as I realized I must say goodbye to him again.

"Would Tau be able to stay with you until I come back?" I asked Mally.

She was turned away from me, rooting inside one of the cupboards, so her voice was muffled. "No," she said, clattering jars and bowls around.

My heart sank. I'd hoped that Mally had warmed to Tau enough to not mind him staying for a few days. There wasn't any other choice then.

"Come on, Tau!" I called, with one hand on the doorframe.

"Wait!" Mally shouted.

"I don't have much time," I said. I could feel the

day seeping through my fingers like sand. Every grain and second was important. "It's already the second day since Kaleb's been missing." *Granny Uma would have found out we'd gone by now.* The guilty thought swirled deep in my stomach.

Mally swiped her braid over her shoulder. "I'm coming with you."

My shoulders sagged in relief. I had thought I was on my own from now on, facing the forest and what lurked in it without a guide or help. "You really want to come?"

Mally nodded. "I've already gathered enough food for a few days. I've also packed herbs and potions for things like snake bites and swamp fever," she said, as if snake bites were as common as midge nibbles.

"Why would you come with me?" I asked her. As happy as I was for the support, I just couldn't think why she'd want to leave the safety of this cottage for the dark and dangerous forest.

"To find Badeko."

"But why would you risk your life for my brother?"

"I want to help you." The lightness in her voice covered something deeper in her words.

What is she up to? But I knew I needed her as a

guide, so I forced down my suspicions and buried them deep.

Mally pulled a crumpled piece of paper out of her pocket. I peered at it. There were charcoal squiggles, with crosses marked along the lines. It wasn't anything that seemed familiar. "What is it?"

"It's a map of all the refuge huts throughout the forest. My papa uses them when he's woodcutting. As long as we're in one of the refuges, the door can be locked at night and we'll be safe. We can use them on the way to the Dead Tree and your brother."

With a nod, she indicated the water pouches.

"Help me fill these up."

I picked one up and dipped it into the pot. The cooling water vapour condensed on the hairs of my arm like mist.

"Won't your parents be worried?" I tied the full water pouch to my pack and began to fill the next one.

Mally heaved her pack on to her shoulders.

"I've left a note," she said, her voice like the sharp edge of a knife, forbidding me from asking more questions.

I followed her outside and pulled the door shut behind us.

The sun had turned the sky from pink dawn to pale blue day. I searched for any sign of clouds but there were none. *It's still early, maybe they will turn up later on.* I whistled for Tau but he had already set off down the path, sniffing at the dry grass, before digging up the roots for his breakfast.

"I'm glad we've got your goat for company," Mally said.

I shook my head. "I wish he wasn't here."

"Why?" Mally squinted at me.

"I feel scared that he will be hurt, which makes me feel weak."

Mally snorted. "You are going to have to learn to be more fearless. You won't save your brother if you're trying to save Tau at the same time. What happens if you have to choose between them?" She raised one eyebrow.

I didn't say anything. I couldn't imagine my life without one or the other.

We walked quickly in the cool morning air. We followed the path that wound through the densewood trees, bare as skeletons, the dry leaves crumbling into dust under our feet. The grass was bleached white as teeth by the sun.

"We have to gain as much ground as we can,

before the sun reaches the middling time. We can get sun sickness if we walk without shade for too long." Mally glanced behind us. "Right now, the sun is still only a quarter way up."

With Mally facing the other direction, I saw them before she did.

"Careful!" I tugged on Mally's dress to stop her treading on the redcap ants. "You almost stepped on them!" The carnivorous insects flowed like a river across the path. They could devour anything that got in their way. *Anything.*

We stood and stared at the huge red ants for a moment, watching as they raced along, crawling over stones, leaves and each other. They were so tightly packed together that they looked like a big headless centipede. Almost every one of them had a leaf or seed on their back.

"They're stocking up on food," I said, an uneasy feeling in my stomach. *I wish the rains would arrive.*

I took a running jump and leaped over the line, even though it was only inches wide. Tau bounded over the ants too. Once he was on the other side, a safe distance away, he stamped his hooves in defiance.

Mally stepped over the line, as if the ants were as harmless as caterpillars.

"Aren't you scared of them?" The thought of getting bitten by a horde of hungry ants made my skin prickle.

She rolled her eyes at me. "If you grow up in a forest, you can't be scared of a few ants!"

I was glad she'd decided to come along with us.

The sun rose higher behind us. Although the branches above the path offered some shade, I could feel the heat gaining strength. It beat down on my head like a hammer.

Mally broke the silence between us. "So, you're from the grasslands?" she said.

"Yes, we live with our Granny Uma. She's a midwife."

"Do you get lonely?" Mally plucked a blade of grass, twirling it between her fingers.

"Not really, I have Kaleb."

"He doesn't count. He's your sibling."

"Siblings do count." I glared at her. "What about you? Do you have a brother or sister?"

"No," Mally said. "I like being by myself." She flicked the blade of grass on to the ground and strode ahead, her braid swinging down her back.

The high sun sapped the energy out of the air, until the birdsong muted and even the midges stopped their hum and nestled into the grass.

It was the middling time of day. The trees grew close enough together to provide some shade. Every so often, I would hear a branch creak, when there was no wind in the heavy air. I searched the trees but there was nothing there. Still, my skin crept with the feeling of being watched.

Instead of stopping for lunch, we ate as we walked. Mally pulled crusty bread out from her pack and I shared one of Granny Uma's goat cheeses.

The taste of the cheese, made from Ela's milk, reminded me of home, and the lake, once full of bream. *Once I've rescued Kaleb and the rains have come, I'll take him to the lake and teach him how to fish. He's old enough to hold a riverwillow rod.*

As if reading my thoughts, Mally asked, "What's your brother's name?"

"Kaleb." With his name came the memories. The sound of him slapping the surface of the lake water and laughing. His laugh sounded like—

I halted. *What had his laugh sounded like?* I tried to bring up the memory of it but I couldn't. There was nothing. A dark cloud had settled over the memory, hiding it from view. Tears pricked the corners of my eyes. *I'm starting to forget him!*

The sun stung my skin but I couldn't move.

I'm losing him.

"It's begun," I croaked. "I'm forgetting things about him."

"We'll find him before the Sorrow Sickness takes hold," Mally said gruffly. "We need to keep moving though."

But I was stuck. A small, secret part of my mind had clung on to the hope that it wasn't true. That Badeko hadn't taken him. That I would find Kaleb safe somewhere, having just wandered off.

Think, Amaya. I focused on the space where his laugh had been, willing the memory back. But I couldn't. It was gone.

The bread and cheese threatened to come back up.

It's real.

Badeko is real and it's taken my small brother.

"I can't remember what his laugh sounds like."

"That's just a small thing."

"No, it isn't." It was a piece of him that was no longer mine. The Dream Eater had stolen it away from me.

"We have to go!" Mally grabbed my arm firmly, snapping me out of myself. "The sun is going to fall soon," she said, glancing upwards. "We still have to cross the river before we get to the refuge hut."

I heard Tau bleat from up ahead. He'd stopped and turned back towards us. When we caught up with him we saw why.

The trail petered out and I saw the mighty river for the first time. But something was wrong. There was no thunder roar of crashing water. No tumbling waves and churning froth.

There was only a river of mud.

The drought had reached the river. The lifeblood of the forest and the grassland.

"This isn't right," Mally stuttered. "The river has never dried up before!" She fumbled with the map. She studied it with her face scrunched up in fierce concentration, then she squinted at the mud, as if that would make the water reappear.

"The drought has killed the river," she wailed. "Without the river, the wells will dry up next. Then the trees will die, and the animals!"

I couldn't believe what I was seeing. *The supply boat. This is why it hasn't made it back.*

"We have to keep going." I had to focus on Kaleb. I grabbed hold of Mally's arms and shook her gently.

"The rains *will* come," I said firmly. "But we have to hurry. The Switching Hour is drawing closer, remember!"

I whistled for Tau, who had been cropping at the yellow grass that grew along the river's edge. He gingerly picked his way on to the mud, took a few steps then sunk to his knees and bleated in alarm. I planted my hands on his backside and heaved. With a *schloooop* he unstuck himself and clambered on to firmer ground. I couldn't help laughing at the dishevelled state of him. There wasn't an inch of his fur that wasn't coated with red dust or mud.

"You look like a river hog," I told him. I started to follow him, but I slipped and landed heavily on my knees. The stench of decay hit the back of my throat and I gagged. The river plants had dried in knots and tangles, still pointing in the direction of the water flow. The skeletal remains of fish floated on the skin of the mud, their bones picked clean and bleached by the sun.

I staggered to my feet and wiped my slimy hands on my tunic.

Above us, the sky was bruised purple and red. The sun was reaching the end of its journey towards the west.

A flock of weaving birds erupted from a needle-thorn tree behind me and as I turned to see the yellow cloud of them twist into the air, something jumped down from the tree.

Long-tailed with a mottled coat, sharp teeth, flashing eyes. The rumbling growl of a predator spying prey.

The wrathclaw cat was back.

Chapter Twelve

"Where are you?"

This time, instinct took over.

"Run!" I shouted to Mally and Tau, hoping they would follow my lead as I tried to pick up my pace. But the sticky, slimy mud clung to my feet, weighing me down, and the smell of rot coated the insides of my mouth and nose. I stopped to spit out the vile taste but the stench from the oozing mud clung to my skin. I could feel it seeping into my pores.

I whipped round and looked for Mally, but she and Tau had disappeared.

"Where are you?" I called out, frantically searching the twilight darkness. I struggled to move my legs, but I only plunged lower, the mud now locking tight around my middle.

Out of the gloom, I saw the stark white sharpness

of fangs as the wrathclaw approached. The cat focused on me, but the mud was also slowing it down. It took its time, as if I was wounded prey.

Confusion muddled my clear thoughts. The light was changing too fast, as day turned into night. I flailed and sank lower into the mud, terror taking over.

"Mally!" I shouted. *What had happened to her?* I shivered as the mud oozed up towards my armpit. My chest felt too tight. In a panic, I tried to scoop the mud away but it flowed like water, filling in the gaps.

The wrathclaw tested the mud with a flick of its paws. It took another step forward.

I couldn't scream. The weight of the mud was too heavy.

I heard a bark. *Tau.* Then the slap of feet on mud as Mally came into view.

"I'm stuck!" I tried to grab hold of her but she backed out of reach. "The wrathclaw, it's coming!"

Why isn't she helping me?

"Stop struggling, you're making it worse!" Mally threw a rope at me. "If you pull me in, we'll both get stuck!"

I grabbed hold of the rope with both hands. It felt springy and soft.

"I cut down a vine from a denseleaf across the river. It should hold." The doubt was clear in her voice.

She tied the other end around Tau's shoulders.

"Pull, Tau!" she cried, and he did. The rope went taut. The mud held on to me with all its might, then with a sucking noise, I slid out and on to firmer ground.

I sat up and groaned. My muddy clothes clung to my skin, leaching cold into my bones. Mally pulled me up into a standing position and I wobbled as if the ground was a tightrope.

"We have to hurry!" I pointed at the wrathclaw, but I couldn't see where it had gone.

A snarl and I spotted it. Its back legs had become trapped into the mud.

Mally pointed up at the sky, which was turning black as a rotten tooth. "The Switching Hour!"

She set off at a fast pace towards the edge of the riverbed. I wrapped the mud-soaked vine around Tau's shoulders and held on to it like a harness as we followed her.

With one last jump, I landed on the edge of the forest.

The wrathclaw.

I saw it struggle in the mud. My heart hurt, even though I was afraid. It was still a living thing. Hunger had made it dangerous.

But with an effort, the wrathclaw freed itself and scrambled for the opposite bank, where it shook the mud from its coat, looking bedraggled and bone thin.

"We have to go." Mally pushed me up the path.

It was then that I saw how little light left there was. The trees were black and grey shadows. The path ahead was a tunnel of darkness.

"How long until we get to the hut?" I whispered.

"Depends on how fast you can run." Mally set off like a hare without looking back. I ran after her, Tau close beside me.

Chapter Thirteen

"Leave him!"

The path twisted and turned around ancient-looking trees, their thick trunks looming like giants in the dark. I ran side by side with Mally, our breathing in time with our feet hitting the ground.

All around us, the forest was stirring. Croaks and squeaks and grumbles that I'd never heard before.

"Faster," Mally panted next to me. "We have to go faster!"

She skidded around another turn in the path, and I threw my arms out to balance myself.

Something moved in the darkness to my left, too fast for my eyes to catch.

"I can see the refuge!" Mally yelled out from just ahead. "Hurry, Amaya!"

The clearing came into view. There was a wooden

hut in the middle of it. I ran towards the refuge, ignoring the searing pain in my side. My lungs felt burned up with fire.

Mally reached the door of the hut first and flung it open. She waved me forward. *We're going to make it!*

Tau bleated in alarm behind me.

My hair whipped in my face and stung my eyes as I turned to look.

"Tau!"

He was stuck. He bucked and kicked, but he was caught. The rope vine that had been wrapped around him to pull me from the mud was tangled in the branches of a needle-thorn tree. His eyes bulged wide as he strained against it.

"Leave him!" Mally yelled from the hut.

"No!" I ran to Tau's side. The vine was caught tight.

"Steady, Tau," I whispered as my fingers fumbled with the mud-encrusted rope. But Tau wouldn't stay still. He bucked wildly and his eyes were rolling in fear.

Then I heard it. The *yip-yip-yip* of hungry voices from the forest path, where we had been moments before. Tau barked short, sharp warnings.

"Please, Tau! Hold still," I begged. One of the knots loosened.

I glanced towards the path. Orange eyes stared

back at me, too many to count. Shadow shapes moved closer on silent paws, the white markings on their backs giving them away.

Daggertooth jackals.

Daggertooths rarely attacked humans. But they were drought-hungry. We were food.

I froze in horror and Mally screamed from the hut. "Move, Amaya! Now!"

In desperation I yanked on the rope, only making the knots bind tighter. The panic-beast had its claws in my brain. I couldn't think. I couldn't move.

I'm going to lose him!

Tau nipped me on the shoulder, hard. "Ow!" I cried.

"Keep breathing," I told myself. *Focus!* I grabbed the end of the vine.

Instead of fighting against it, I followed the path of the rope. *Through the loop, over the branch, under Tau.* It loosened and gave way.

Tau gave a kick and he was free.

"Run!" Mally screamed.

I grabbed hold of Tau's collar. We ran, Tau almost dragging me off my feet.

Mally held the door open and we both stumbled inside.

We'd made it! I tried to catch my breath, but my

heart was hammering and adrenaline flooded through me.

"The jackals have gone," Mally said, still holding the door open a sliver.

"Close the door, Mally!"

Mally stood, silent, gripping the door with white knuckles.

"Something's scared them away," she whispered.

I shoved her to one side and slammed the door shut, sliding the lock into place before flinging my arms around Tau's neck and pressing my face against his fur.

Tau tried to clamber on to my lap, like he would when he was small, but he was now the size of a boulder and almost as heavy. I gently heaved him off.

"You're a brave goat," I told him.

Then I turned on Mally. "Why didn't you help me free Tau? We need to stick together – you just ran in here and hid!"

Mally flung kindling into the hearth, her face furious. "I rescued you from the mud and the wrathclaw, didn't I? Anyway, why should I care about anyone else?" She struck the flint against the steel of her tinderbox. Almost too low for me to hear, she added, "Nobody cares about me."

"I *did* care about you until you abandoned me and Tau to the jackals!"

"I was going to help, but I was waiting until Badeko appeared." Mally blinked into the fire. Her red hair hung in matted strings. She looked like a wild thing. "I want to find it! I *need* to find it."

"We're looking for my brother!" I shouted. "What reason do you have to find Badeko so desperately?"

"I said I would help you and that's what I'm doing." Mally snapped a stick over her knee with a crack. "Badeko would have come out of hiding if you'd left Tau for a moment longer."

"You used us as bait?" *How could she be so heartless?*

"The quicker we find Badeko, the quicker we find your brother." Mally glared at me. "Or don't you care enough about finding him in time?"

"How dare you accuse me of not caring!" Anger turned my words into a hiss. My skin burned up with heat and my nails bit into my palm. Without thinking, I moved towards her with closed fists.

Mally raised her hand. "Don't move!" she whispered. Her eyes were fixated on the woodpile which she'd been using to build the fire.

She stepped back carefully from the logs, her eyes never leaving the spot.

"What is it?" I craned my neck towards the woodpile. I caught a scuttle of movement. A flash of black and red, the size of a mouse. But it had too many legs to be a mouse...

Chapter Fourteen

"Is there no other way?"

"A spider?" I stepped forward. "The fearless forest dweller is afraid of spiders!" I mocked, the anger still boiling under my skin.

Mally grabbed my arm, pulling me away from the woodpile.

"Get off me!" I snatched my arm away, but I didn't go any closer. Mally's eyes were wide.

"Mally, what is it?" I said. "What's wrong?"

"It's a nightcrawler spider."

"I don't know what that is," I admitted. *I wish I'd studied Granny Uma's forest books while I had the chance.*

"It's the most venomous spider in the forest!" Mally glared at me, as if it was my fault the spider was there. "If you get bitten, you'll die."

My mouth went dry. I grabbed hold of Tau's collar.

"There's a nest of them in the woodpile." Mally pointed, just as two spiders scuttled out from between the logs. They were black with red patches on their backs and they probed the air with hairy legs in the direction of the fire. Their shadows against the light cast by the flames made them look twice as big.

My skin broke out in a cold sweat.

We jumped back, keeping as much distance between us and them as the hut wall would allow. The room felt too small all of a sudden.

"What are we going to do?" I found myself whispering.

"We can't stay here, not with those things in the room," replied Mally.

I glanced at her in alarm. "But we can't go back out there!"

"We don't have a choice!" Mally hadn't looked away from the woodpile.

But Badeko was out there!

"Is there no other way?"

Mally puffed out her cheeks, not letting her gaze slip away from the woodpile. "If we can find a yellowbark tree, we can rub the sap into our skin. The spiders will stay clear of us then and we can sleep inside the hut until the sun comes up. I thought I saw one, back down the trail. It was dark, but I recognized the jagged leaves." She pushed me towards the door. "We have to go back outside, just for a few minutes."

I protested, still holding on to Tau's collar.

Mally kept shoving me until we were through the door. "Trust me, we'll all be dead by morning if we don't get the sap."

I stepped outside. *This doesn't feel right.* Every nerve in my body screamed to go back inside. Granny Uma's voice echoed in my head. *Don't let the outside in!* She'd be furious to see us walking around outside at night, after the Switching Hour. But she wasn't here to stop us.

I was suddenly aware of how alone we really were.

Nothing could be heard apart from the crickets and a nightjar shriek in the distance.

"Come on," Mally urged. "We have to be quick."

The hairs on my arms stood up. My eyes fixed on the shadows between the trees, seeking any movement. With a shiver, I imagined eyes watching us from every angle.

"What if the jackals come back?" My voice was a whisper, full of fear.

Mally didn't answer, just motioned for me to follow her.

Reluctantly, I trailed Mally along the track, back the way we'd come. At least the moon was in its waxing phase, growing bigger each night, so we could pick out our path. I was glad of Tau now; his scratchy fur against my arm was reassuring. I felt braver with him beside me.

The chirrup of a bat. I flinched, thinking it was another one of Badeko's hallucinations, but it swooped and snatched a moth that Tau had stirred up from the grass alongside the path, before flying away.

"You're grinding your teeth," Mally hissed. "Stop it, I can't concentrate!"

My jaw ached. I opened and closed my mouth. "Sorry," I mumbled. The outside was getting to me. I felt too exposed. Everything was a threat.

The mournful cry of a nightwarbler made me jolt. An answering cry from a faraway bird and then they both fell silent.

The night smelled different to the day. As if we'd stepped into another world, one where we didn't belong. Everything felt sharper, more alive. More watchful.

"Are we getting close?" I whispered, but even so the words felt too loud.

I searched each tree, looking for one with jagged leaves. But all the trees were bare, their branches dark snakes across the starry sky. They all looked the same to me.

The lake and open grasslands were my home; here I was a stranger.

I was curious how Mally knew so much about the forest.

"Did your papa teach you about the trees?" I asked her.

She nodded. "He said I had to adapt to the forest, not force the forest to adapt to us." She stopped, peering up at a large tree with a sprawling canopy. "Didn't your papa teach you about the forest?"

"No," I said. "He left before my brother was born. My mama and Granny Uma looked after us."

"It was the opposite for me." She tapped her chin, concentrating on the branches above. "It was my papa who took care of me."

"What do you mean?" *I thought her mama was in the Eastern Town with her papa?*

Mally pulled at her hair, untucking it from behind her ear. I had to strain to hear her say,

133

"My real mama died when I was little. It was only Papa and me for most of my growing up, before he married someone else."

I could tell it was the truth because of the way it seemed to hurt Mally to say the words. Lies came much more easily to her, the words slippery like snakes.

Before I could reply, Mally put out her hand to stop me. She motioned upwards.

This tree was the only one with a few jagged leaves still clinging to the branches. The moonlight picked out the leaf skeleton, bleached translucent by the sun.

"What now?" I pressed my hand to the trunk. The bark was warm.

Mally slid her knife out of her belt pocket. The blade flashed.

I took a step backwards, reaching out for Tau.

With a grunt, Mally plunged the knife into the tree, up to the hilt. With an effort, she jiggled the knife up and down and pulled it loose. Clear liquid oozed out of the hole, filling the air with a sweet smell that caught at the back of my throat, making me cough.

"Cover your skin with it." Mally had already

started swiping the sap off the tree and rubbing it on to her legs.

I poked my finger on to the sap, expecting it to be sticky, but it soaked into my skin like milk, leaving behind the smell of overripe fruit, sickly-sweet.

I scooped a handful and brushed it over my arm, surprised how soft and warm it felt.

Mally kneaded it into her hair, coating the strands. I did the same.

"It's the smell that repels the spiders; as long as we've got enough of it into our skin, it should last the night."

I turned to Tau. "Your turn."

Tau seemed to enjoy having the sap rubbed into his fur. He leaned into the back scratch, not caring that it made him smell like a sugar cube.

Mally dribbled some of the sap into an empty wooden box and then tied it back on to her belt. "We'll make a sap circle around our sleeping area, to be extra careful."

The moon was high above us; we'd been outside for too long.

"We need to get back." My eyes searched the branches above us for movement. A wood owl croaked, sounding like an old toad. I caught the white blur of wings as it flew from one tree to the next.

We started back, Tau leading us down the path. Soon, the refuge hut came into sight and I breathed out in relief. We'd made it.

The clearing was silver bright. I glanced up, but there were no clouds.

The stars covered the sky like nettle rash.

"Let's get inside," Mally whispered. She half-turned back towards me, when something caught her eye, freezing her to the spot.

"What is it?" I could only hear the shrill cricket noise. I squinted at the darkness between the needle-thorn trees, my skin prickling.

Was something there? A shadow watching us?

The shadow moved.

A daggertooth jackal stepped into the clearing, a growl low in its throat.

"Let's get inside, Mally." I tugged on her sleeve.

She pulled away. "It can't be," she murmured, staring at the daggertooth.

Only then did I realize the creature was too small to be a daggertooth, and its dark fur didn't have the white stripes running down its back.

It barked.

"It's a dog!" I wondered what it was doing so far

into the forest. Its tail wagged in a friendly way.

"Hunter?" Mally's voice trembled.

Surprised, I asked her, "Do you know this dog?"

"He was mine."

"He was?"

"He died a year ago," she whispered.

My pulse quickened.

"We have to get inside, Mally." I reached out, but she spun away.

Tau bleated, unnerved by the creature that had appeared in the clearing. I instinctively put my hand on his collar.

"Hunter?" She walked towards the dog. "Is that you?"

"No, Mally!" I followed her without thinking. "It's a trick!" Even as I said it, the dog was changing. It was growing bigger with each step Mally took towards it. Its legs morphed into eight spindly limbs that picked their way towards us. *This can't be real.* Everything looked and felt wrong, as if the world had been tipped upside down.

Tau backed away towards the cottage, half-dragging me with him, but I couldn't leave Mally behind.

Mally reached towards the dog, her palm out. "Come here, Hunter!" She laughed like a toddling.

She stood in the clearing, barefoot, her red hair almost white from the moon's light.

I grabbed her other arm. "It's not Hunter!"

The dog barked, but all I could hear was the song. It hummed through the teeth of the dog with eight legs. The song spun like silk from the air and tangled up my thoughts.

I was aware of the dry grass under my feet, tickling my ankles. The cool night air sliding over the hairs on my arms and rustling the dry leaves on the trees.

I could just let go. Let the song take me.

Let Badeko bring me to Kaleb.

I dug my nails into Mally's arm.

Mally yelped, then turned to me, her green eyes full of confusion.

"We have to get inside!" I wondered if I'd said the words out loud. I couldn't tell.

I looked at the dog. I could see the adoration in its eyes as it stared up at Mally. Despite its monstrous body, its face looked so harmless.

Clever Badeko.

Her fingers still outstretched, Mally reached towards the shapeshifting creature.

I tore my gaze away and dragged Mally off, the

ground feeling as unstable as the mud had earlier. With each step, a song-thread was severed and my head grew clearer, less full of fog.

With Tau by my side, I reached the door and pulled Mally into the hut, slamming the bolt down with a crash.

This time there was no way I was letting anyone open it again.

Chapter Fifteen

"You have me and Tau now"

Mally sank to the floor. "That was Hunter – my dog, Hunter!" Tears were tumbling down her cheeks. "I miss him so much." It was jarring to see strong, brittle Mally this undone.

I kneeled down next to her and put my arm around her shoulders. "Couldn't you see the dog had eight legs?" I asked gently.

She blinked rapidly. "No! He looked the same as he always had."

Tau trotted over and snuffled her hair. Mally tried to push him away, but he curled up next to her with his head resting on her knee. She gave in and wrapped her arms around his neck.

The sickly smell of the tree sap filled the room. It was like breathing in syrup. I glanced at the woodpile but there was no sign of the spiders. The sap must be working.

Mally gently moved Tau from her lap and got up. With the sap, she drew a wide circle around the three of us. It seeped into the stone floor, glistening amber in the firelight.

"What happened to Hunter?" I asked softly.

"He was old when he died." Mally swiped at her eyes with her sleeve. "He was my papa's dog. When I was born, Hunter decided he liked me best." She gave me a wobbly smile. "He was my best friend."

I remembered what she'd said about liking her own company, and wondered how much of what she told me was true.

But Badeko knew everything about us, from our dreams and our nightmares. I tried not to think about the monster he had just conjured up from Mally's mind.

"You have me and Tau now," I told Mally.

To my shock, Mally dissolved into tears again. She pressed her forehead against her raised knees, her shoulders shaking.

Mally was my fearless guide, who could cure snake bites and trick deadly nightcrawler spiders.

I didn't know what to say to make her feel better. "I'll get us something to eat."

I stood up and stepped over the sap line, feeling like the first time I'd set foot in the forest – that I was walking into danger.

The cloying, sweet smell of the sap was enough to give me a dull headache, so I hoped the spiders would hide away from it all night. But still, my eyes snagged on every flicker of firelight shadow, conjuring up long legs and scuttling bodies.

I wandered around the small room, with Tau sniffing into every corner.

It was bare apart from a table, three chairs and two beds. I went over and prodded the mattresses with my foot and caught a whiff of mould. Straw poked through the canvas mattress and Tau took a nibble at it. He hacked a cough.

"That straw is probably a thousand years old, Tau," I tutted.

I found two chipped ceramic plates in the kitchen cupboard, covered with dust. I wiped each one on my sleeve and brought it back to the fireplace, making sure to step over the line of sap.

"Take this." I tapped Mally lightly on her

shoulder. She raised her head, swiping at her eyes before taking the plate from me.

I rummaged in my bag and brought out some cheese, slicing it thinly on to each plate.

Mally only picked at her portion, even though she hadn't eaten much today. I handed her some bread to go with it, breaking off the crusts first and giving her the softer insides.

"You have to eat something," I coaxed. "We've got a long walk tomorrow."

"The bread is stale." Mally knocked it against her plate. "See?"

"Doesn't matter, you have to eat it." *I sound just like Granny Uma.* The thought made my throat tighten. *She'll be so worried about me and Kaleb.* I pushed the guilt to the back of my mind. I had to stay strong.

Thankfully, Mally did what I said, chewing each bite as if it was torment. I couldn't help but smile at her grimaces. Mally even smiled back, in a way that made her whole face brighter.

When she'd finished, she passed me the empty plate and stuck out her tongue at me. "I ate it all, even though it tasted like rocks."

"Have you ever eaten rocks?" I teased.

"No, but that's probably what they taste like." She

dusted the crumbs off her dress into the fire. She looked happier now she'd eaten something.

I wondered again why she had spoken to the vision of her dead dog, Hunter. She had asked it something, but my tired brain couldn't remember what she'd said. The smell of the sap, the fire-warmth and the food in my stomach made the urge to sleep too powerful to resist.

I yawned and stretched, glancing at the woodpile. Despite the sap circle, it still felt risky sleeping in a room of poisonous spiders. *What if the sap stopped working?*

"We'll head to the next refuge tomorrow. It's the one nearest the Dead Tree," Mally abruptly said, as if carrying on a previous conversation.

The Dead Tree. Where I'll find my brother. I pressed my fingers to my temple, my head feeling as heavy as lead.

A movement in the corner of the room made me jump. I watched, transfixed, as a spider the size of my hand inched out between the logs. It stopped, raising its front legs in the air, then retreated with terrifying speed. The sap was working.

"That's really clever of you, to know how to ward off the spiders," I said to Mally, feeling real warmth towards her. "I'm glad you decided to come with us."

Mally shrugged her shoulders as if it was nothing, but I saw the pleased smile that pulled at the corners of her mouth.

"I mean it! I wouldn't have lasted long in the forest without you."

Mally fiddled with the hem of her dress. "Well, I thought it was brave, what you did," she replied. "Rescuing Tau from the jackals."

I glanced down at Tau, who was curled up next to me, his eyes closed and his head on my knee. My heart tugged at the sight of him. All the memories piled up, of Tau as a goatling, all knobbly knees and long droopy ears. When he was very young and sickly he'd slept on my bed despite Granny Uma's grumbles, and I'd woken up throughout the night to comfort him. Since then, he'd been my shadow.

I couldn't imagine my life without him in it.

"I'm not brave. I'm just too scared of losing him." Deep down I knew Mally understood; she must have felt the same about Hunter.

"I've never met a goat that acted like a dog before." Mally reached out and scratched the dip between Tau's horns, making his long eyelashes flutter in his sleep. "He's very special."

"You should meet his mama and papa when we get back home." I felt a surge of excitement. "Ela is beautiful and brave and Zola's horns are as big as tree branches!" I couldn't wait to show Mally our cottage, the lake and the goats.

"Once we've found Badeko, I can come and meet them," she said.

The words were friendly, but I couldn't shake the feeling that Mally was missing something out, something important.

"But we need to rescue Kaleb first."

"Who's Kaleb?" Her confusion was real.

"My brother." I said it firmly, but my heart was thundering. I was suddenly afraid. "You're forgetting him!"

Mally put her hand on my shoulder and I realized I was shaking. "I never met him, so there's nothing there to forget," she said gently. "I'm not going to be able to hold on to the memory of him, not while Badeko has him and is eating his dreams."

"Does that mean you'll just keep forgetting that I've got a brother?" I couldn't keep the tremble out of my voice.

"I haven't built up any memories of him, not like you have," Mally said.

The weight of responsibility felt too heavy to carry. *What if I forget him? He'll be lost for ever!*

Mally jumped up and pulled the woollen blankets off the beds, shaking them, before bringing them over to the hearth, where the fire was now just flickers of heat. As she wrapped them around me, I felt the panic-beast claw at my stomach, shoving its way into my chest. Tau sneaked into the folds and snuggled up against my back. I leaned against him.

Mally curled up beside me. "Tell me about your brother," she said. "It will help you remember him more clearly."

I couldn't help but smile. "He's like a little goat. He won't keep still for a moment, only when he's asleep does he stop." I thought of the chaos that followed him everywhere. "Kaleb always wants to explore and climb and mess everything up."

Mally frowned. "He sounds naughty. I don't know if I would like that."

"He just wants to be a part of everything. He loves the goats, and the chickens, and playing in the vegetable garden. He helps Granny Uma pick the cabbages and the yams." *Although helping wasn't quite the right word*, I thought, remembering the scolding he'd got from Granny Uma when he pulled up all the seedlings.

"Did you miss being the only child?" Mally leaned towards me. "Was it better before he was born?"

"It wasn't better, just different," I said, too quickly. *Had it been better? When it was just Mama and me? Before Kaleb took up all her energy and time?*

"Did your mama ignore you, after he was born?" Mally asked insistently. I could see my face reflected in her green eyes, she was staring so intently at me.

"Maybe when he was still a baby and needed Mama all the time," I said truthfully. "It was hard, when I wanted Mama's attention and she was too tired to talk to me. I sometimes missed the time when it was just us two."

Mally nodded. "That's what I thought."

"But I loved being a sister!" My heart thudded at the slip into past tense. "I just wish I'd realized how much, before he was taken."

Mally stared into the fire, her mouth downturned. "We should get some sleep," she said.

The three of us curled up together. I rested my hand on Tau's side and felt the rise and fall of his stomach.

"Thank you for earlier." Mally turned to face me. "For saving me from that horrible creature pretending to be poor Hunter."

"It was nothing," I grinned. "I save people from scary spider-dogs all the time."

Mally did an exaggerated eye roll. She was *very* good at doing those. "I'm sure you do."

The fire had died down and the room was full of heat. My eyelids felt so heavy.

"Can you sing that rhyme?" Mally whispered.

I felt my cheeks heat up, realizing she had heard me singing the night before.

"Please?" she begged.

And so, under my breath, I sang the bedtime rhyme.

Close your eyes and breathe in deep
It's time for you to go to sleep
Until the moon has gone to hide
I will be right by your side.

I was exhausted, but even so the fear of nightmares made the thought of sleep terrifying. I snuggled closer to Tau and caught the smell of Mally's hair, woodchips and aloe leaves, almost hidden under the stink of sap.

At least I wasn't alone.

The creature snuffled under the door. The dreams were thick and heavy, they pooled in the humid night air like syrup and honey.

It could taste the Fire Dreamer. She was dreaming of a time before. The creature could taste hope turned to ash. A fear so sour that it grimaced, its lips pulled back from sharp teeth. Never had it tasted dreams like this, so full of flavour and fire.

The Lonely One also slept and dreamed, it could taste the salt-crystal secrets that encrusted her heart, drying it up. It longed to crunch on the dream, splintering it into pieces.

The creature knew the dreams from the boy wouldn't last much longer. It needed to capture the Fire Dreamer before its strength began to ebb.

Chapter Sixteen

"He smells like blood"

The pain cracked through the surface of the dream and wrenched me into wakefulness.

Lightning bolts recoiled inside my skull and sparked against my eyelids. The headaches were getting worse. I wondered if it was to do with Kaleb's dreams being eaten and my memories along with them.

I squeezed my eyes tightly shut. The dream was still muddling up my thoughts. It had been a nightmare of flame and choking smoke, which cleared to a great emptiness, leaving me drained and trembling. The ache from missing Mama beat against the inside of my chest.

Tau stirred but didn't wake. I leaned my forehead against his back. The warmth of his fur was soothing and the headache evaporated, leaving me feeling shaky but relieved.

I sat up and peered around the room. It was early but I could tell it would soon be dawn from the way the dark was weakening. Mally was still asleep. Her hair spilled out from between the folds of the blanket.

The sickly smell of the sap coated my throat. I glanced at the woodpile, but there was no movement from the spiders. *Mally's trick with the sap had worked!* The realization that I wouldn't have lasted this long without her made me shiver.

My whole body felt heavy with tiredness; I must have only skimmed the surface of sleep. But I couldn't rest any longer – now that I was awake, all I could think about was Kaleb.

I wished there was a way to let him know that I was on my way.

I folded my knees up against my chest. I closed my eyes.

I remembered seeing my brother for the first time.

Mama had called me into her room. The small space had smelled like sunburned skin and sweat, even though the window was fully open.

Rain had been late that year as well. Every year the rains had been later and later and the summer hotter and hotter. The warmth from the sun poured into the room.

Granny Uma held a tiny bundle of cotton cloth in her arms. "Meet your brother, Amaya!" She'd parted the cloth for me to see.

I'd stared at his scrunched-up face. He had smelled of woodchips and stembark flowers. And something else. Something fearful.

"He smells like blood," I'd said and backed away.

Granny Uma hadn't disagreed. "He needs a bath." She handed the bundle back to Mama, then began filling a tub with water warmed on the stove. The steam filled the room.

"Come here, small daughter." Mama reached towards me, stretching out across the distance between us. I hesitated for a moment, then I ran into her one-armed embrace. She hugged me as tight as if she had two arms free.

"This is your small brother. His name is Kaleb." She didn't look away from me. "I want you to promise to care for him." Her eyes were too bright. It was like looking into the sun.

"I promise."

Mama smiled and her eyes softened. "Now, take him to Granny Uma for his bath. I need some rest." She showed me how to hold him, with my arm supporting his neck.

He studied me with eyes that seemed too big. Almost big enough to fill the empty space left by Papa, who had walked away one night and never come back.

"Hello, small brother," I whispered.

The memory faded and I opened my eyes. I felt the wetness of tears on my cheeks but I didn't brush them away. *I've broken Mama's promise.*

I heard the first day-birds start to wake up, and I stood, careful not to disturb Tau or Mally. The earth floor felt cold under my feet as I walked to the window, where I peered out, searching for signs of the sun through the trees.

It was the Switching Hour. The moon was skulking back to its lair under the horizon and the sun was stretching out its arms. The sky was divided into gold and grey.

A movement caught my eye. Something was in the clearing.

It was a shadow, shifting in shape like a creature within a dark sackcloth bag, trying to escape.

I squinted and pressed my face against the crack in the wood.

It moved into the morning sun. As it moved, the shape of nothingness filled with light. It shimmered and transformed. Where there had been a shadow there was now a reflection. A person with dark hair and darker eyes. It was a person that I knew like my own self.

My breath rushed out. "Mama," I whispered.

I ran to the door and fumbled for the lock but my hand was slapped away.

"What are you doing?" Mally hissed. "The Switching Hour isn't over yet!"

I ignored her. I reached for the lock again but Mally grabbed my arm.

"No, Amaya!" She wrapped both arms around me and heaved me away from the door. She was a lot stronger than me, but I struggled and kicked out.

"It's my mama!" I wheezed. Mally was squeezing too tight. "My mama's outside!"

Mally eased her grip but didn't let me go. "I thought your mama was…" She didn't finish but her hold on me relaxed. Enough for me to struggle free and grab the lock. With a click the bolt loosened and I swung the door open.

I stepped into the clearing.

"Mama?" I whispered.

"Amaya!" Her voice sounded far away, yet so close it felt as if the words were already inside my head, waiting to be unlocked at this exact moment in time.

She smiled, and the creases around her eyes were the same. Every line, every detail was perfect. The empty space was gone.

"Is it *really* you?" I swallowed around the rattle of fear in my throat.

Instinctively, I knew that this vision understood every part of me. It knew everything I'd ever done, everything I'd ever said. It knew me, like a mother knows her own daughter. But its eyes weren't Mama's.

I could see a hunger there.

The hunger became my own; my belly ached with it, a strong tug that pulled me towards the shape of my mama. The memories came flooding back.

I remembered how she'd brush my hair softly, being careful of the knots and tangles, all the while scolding me for not tying it up properly. The smell of the laundry soap on her hands, the wood-bark on her clothes from chopping up firewood for the stove. Her belly laugh that made me laugh too. Her singing voice that sent me off to sleep, safe knowing she was watching over me. It hurt to remember those memories, exposing the emptiness where she used to be.

"I miss you so much, Mama!"

I could stop fighting. I could just let those painful memories go. No more nightmares.

Give them to Badeko.

A hand yanked me backwards, snapping me awake.

Mally grabbed my shoulder. I tried to shrug her off but she wrapped her arms around me.

"It's not your mama," she whispered.

"It looks just like her," I said, but the tears had found their way into my throat and I choked on the words. The shape was beginning to evaporate as the light grew stronger.

Please don't go!

"We need to go back inside, Amaya," Mally said. "It isn't safe."

I took one more look at the face that was so wonderful. The face I saw every night in my dreams.

The shadow shape of my mama reached out across the space between us.

"Amaya," it said in Mama's voice. But I knew

Mally was right. It wasn't her – this was Badeko's cruelty.

I turned and let Mally guide me back into the house, blinded by my tears.

Once inside, Mally slammed the door shut. I heard the bolt click into place. She pulled me towards the hearth and sat me down beside Tau, who curled up against my side.

"That was a horrible trick," Mally said angrily. She sat down next to me.

"It looked just like my mama." The memories had overwhelmed me, yanking me back to the past when everything had been fine. Now I was trapped in the present without Mama or Kaleb.

"Do you want to tell me what happened to her?"

I wiped my wet face on my scarf. "We used to live in the Eastern Town," I said quietly. "I went swimming at the lake. Mama had been so tired with Kaleb just being born; Granny Uma was looking after Kaleb, taking him on her rounds, checking in on another new mama. But my Mama must have left the stove door open by mistake. An ember started a fire that spread to the thatch." My throat felt dry. "Mama was sleeping inside when it burned down." The old itchy thought resurfaced. *If Mama hadn't*

160

been so tired, she would have woken up in time. I refused to scratch it. "Ever since she's been gone, I've been afraid of the empty space."

Mally frowned. "What space?"

"The empty space that's eating up my memories of her." I tried to make Mally understand. "The forgetfulness that's destroying the memory of my mama." *And now the empty space is eating up the memory of my small brother.*

Mally stood and pulled me to my feet.

"It's time to go," she said. "We're going to find your brother and bring him home."

After breakfast, I packed up my bag, counting out the millet grain, a small chunk of goat's cheese and a rock of stale bread. *We don't have enough food to last the journey there and back.* I shoved the thought to the back of my mind. Right now, my only goal was to find Kaleb.

A golden glint from the bottom of my bag snatched my attention. *My tinderbox.*

I pulled it out, seeing the indent of my name. I pressed my thumb down on the engraving, forcing the mark on to my skin for a moment before it faded back into the lines of my fingerprint. It made my heart stronger, to *feel* the name that Mama had given me.

"Amaya!" Mally called. She waved me over, the map open in her hands. I slipped the tinderbox into the pocket of my tunic and joined her.

"Which way?" I asked, peering over her shoulder. Her finger followed the path that snaked around the hut and led deeper into the forest. She jabbed at a red cross.

"We're a day's journey from the next refuge point," she said. "It's the last refuge hut before the centre of the forest. If we get there tonight, we'll be close enough to head to the Dead Tree at first light tomorrow."

Mally pushed the map to the bottom of her pack.

We left the hut, with the smell of the sap still lingering inside. It felt good to breathe clean air again.

"Tau!" I called out and the goat came running. We walked away from the clearing and followed the path.

I counted the days I had been in the forest. "Today is the third day since my brother was taken," I said.

"What's his name?" Mally asked.

"Kaleb," I said, hating that she had already forgotten. "You're not going to be able to remember."

"No, not while Badeko has him," Mally said

regretfully. "But I can keep asking, to help you remember."

We followed the path further into the forest. The light was pale and almost frosty, but the sun would soon rise above the treeline to change all that.

"How much can you remember of him?" Mally asked.

"I remember him as a baby," I said, thinking of the morning's memory. "But I don't remember him as a toddling." I dug my nails into my palms to try and stop the panic that was twisting my stomach into knots. I knew that he *was* a toddling, at least, but nothing more than that. *What words did he know? Was he quiet or loud? What colour were his eyes?*

Mally nudged me with her shoulder, pulling me out of my thoughts.

"It's OK. There is time. As long as you can remember that he exists, there is time," she said. The calmness in her voice quieted the panic-beast in my stomach.

We walked fast along the path; the bouncing of my pack matched the rhythm of my footfalls. Hungry grasshoppers were gathering in the grass that lined the path, and the dry and yellow clumps reverberated with their song.

The ground cracked with the heat, and our feet scuffed up red dust that settled on our leg and arm hairs. My throat itched with the taste of dirt that turned my saliva into a paste. I longed for a dip in the lake.

We came into a clearing and I stared up at the sky, searching for any clouds.

"I wish the rain would arrive," I croaked. The sky was so blue it made my eyes hurt to look at it.

"This has been the longest drought we've ever had," Mally said, through gritted teeth.

I thought of the pasture grass at home, dry and yellow. If the thunderstorms held off for much longer, we would lose our grazing land. *What would happen to Zola, Ela and Tau?* My taste buds ached with the memory of eating the tangy sunfruit that had thrived after last year's rains. We'd had more of the fruit than we knew what to do with, turning it into pies, stews and delicious juice. I tried to focus on something else.

I fumbled for the stone in my pocket, but only a piece of charcoal wood was hidden there.

With a sickening lurch of my stomach, I realized Mama's stone was gone. I halted in the middle of the path, Tau bumping against my legs.

I threw the contents of my bag on to the ground and rooted through them. Sand stuck to the cheese and the bread and my scarf was tangled up into knots, but I couldn't find the stone.

"What are you doing?" Mally asked, walking over to us.

"It's gone," I gasped, digging around in case it had got buried, the hot sand burning my fingers. It wasn't there.

It must have fallen out of my pocket while I was saving Tau.

"We have to go back!" I shovelled everything back into the bag, covered in dirt and sand.

"We'll never make it to the next refuge hut if we don't keep moving!"

"You don't understand." My throat was tight. "I've lost the stone, Mama's stone!"

"What stone?"

"I'll forget the colour of her eyes without it!" I sobbed dry heaves that rasped painfully against my throat, hating myself for it. "I'll lose *her*!"

"You're not going back to try and find a stone," Mally said firmly. "We need to find your *brother*, remember?"

"I'll forget her," was all I could say.

"It doesn't matter if you forget the colour of her eyes. You won't forget *her*," Mally told me, grabbing my arm and hauling me forward.

I let her lead me, but it felt as though I was leaving fragments of myself behind. Memories lost in the dirt and dust. *Will there be anything left of me by the time I get to the Dead Tree?* I gripped hold of Tau's collar. *At least he will still be by my side.*

All around us, the air was still. There was no wind disturbing the clatterpod trees; the long, brown seed pods hung heavy and silent. It felt like the forest had entered a deep sleep, slowly crumbling back into the ground. If the rains didn't arrive soon, there would be nothing left but dust.

We took sips from the water pouch. Occasionally, Tau would stop and dig up the roots of the woody shrubs, but once he uncovered them, I could see that the tubers had shrivelled into almost nothingness. Tau seemed content to snack on them anyway.

The sun climbed higher and the ground heated up. We jumped like frogs from shadow to shadow, but soon the sun reached the middling point. The baked soil burnt the soles of our feet.

"We have to wait out the heat," Mally gasped. "We can shelter in the shadow of the needle-thorn tree."

I followed the imprint of her footprints, but it felt like walking on hot coals.

The needle-thorn tree was the perfect shape. The canopy stretched outwards and even without the leaves, the branches offered a crisscross of shade. Once underneath, I dug my toes into the cooler dirt.

"How long do we have to wait?" I asked Mally. She was leaning against the tree, using her pack as a buffer against the cracked bark. She glanced upwards and squinted at the dappled light.

"We'll have to wait until the sun has started to fall towards the west." She yawned and shut her eyes. "Just rest. We'll make up the time when the ground is cooler."

Her lips were cracked, and her cheeks burned red. I was worried about her. I had lived my life in the grasslands, where the sun had always been fierce, no matter the season. But Mally was used to the shade of the forest, the trees' protection.

While she slept, I swept the dirt off my feet, searching for blisters. The skin there was usually as tough as buffalo hide, but now it was tender to the touch. I clicked my tongue. My left big toe had a white blister. *It could be worse.*

The sun slowly moved over the top of the needle-thorn.

I gnawed my nails; my teeth crunched the grit that hid underneath them. It felt wrong, to be sitting still while it was daylight. But I knew Mally was right. When the ground cooled, we would be able to run, instead of hobbling from shadow to shadow.

Tau dug a small hole in the soil then curled up in the dust. His fur was no longer white – he looked more like a red river hog than a goat.

With a sharp *crack,* I snapped a twig from an overhead branch.

I bent down and drew pictures in the dust with the stick. With a trembling hand, I sketched the outline of Mama's profile: her jaw, her hair and her nose. The stick broke, so I traced her eye and her smile with my finger. *I will find another stone, one the exact colour of your eyes. I won't forget*, I promised her. With her face in the sand, I felt better and started to draw Kaleb but hesitated. *How could I draw my small brother when I couldn't remember what he looked like?* The panic-beast woke up, gnawing at my stomach. Instead, I quickly traced around my handprint in the soil; then I drew a smaller hand inside it. *Me and my small brother.*

I wondered how Kaleb was, as he slept in the hollow of the Dead Tree. *Is he hurt? Is he scared?* The waiting piled on pressure in my chest and made me restless. I paced around the shadow line of the tree, pounding a circle in the dirt.

Tau woke up. He stretched the kinks out of his neck and shook his horns, creating a small dust cloud from his beard.

"You must be thirsty," I said. I poured water into the hollow of my hand so he could drink and he licked it dry.

I sipped the water from the pouch and picked at some hard cheese. The heat and the anxious waiting had stolen the hunger from my belly, but I knew I had to eat. The crumbs of cheese stuck to the back of my throat and tasted bitter and gritty.

Mally jolted awake. For a heartbeat, I saw her eyes fill with confusion, then she rubbed her face, leaving red dust on her eyelashes.

I handed her the water pouch and some of the cheese and bread. She took a sip but grimaced at the food. When she reluctantly handed the water pouch back, I placed it on the ground.

"Are you OK?" I asked.

Mally was quiet for a moment. I could see her

wrestling with her thoughts. I knew her well enough now to know that she didn't like to let them go easily.

"I miss my papa. Or, I miss how things were when it was just the two of us." Mally scuffed the dirt with her heel. "Everything was fine, until Papa got married again."

"Who did he marry?"

"She's an artist and her name's Sadi. She tries too hard to be nice." Mally scowled, dirt lining the furrows in her brow. "She wants to be my new mama, but she isn't."

"What was your mama like?" I asked her.

Mally rested her chin on her hand. "She had a kind voice. She used to sing me to sleep." Mally reached down and drew a circle in the dust at her feet. "Mama used to laugh a lot. She talked even more." Mally lost her careful tone, and now the words flowed like a stream. "I remember her voice as if it was music, even though the words are lost. Mama would sing, and Papa would whistle along because he said he didn't have the voice for singing, not like Mama did." Mally smiled.

"Do you remember what she looked like?"

"No, I don't."

"Are you sad that you can't remember?" I asked.

I glanced at the face I'd drawn in the sand. The fear of the empty space taking my mama from me filled me with panic.

Mally shook her head. "Memory isn't just about what you see; it's how you feel. Like how my mama made me feel safe and loved."

She drew three interlocking circles in the dust, and I examined the handprints I'd drawn earlier. *We all have our own way of remembering the people we miss.*

Mally glanced up at the sky and reached for her pack. "It's past the middling time. We can carry on."

She stood up, wriggling her backpack on.

"Oh no," she said.

"What?" I snapped my head up, searching for signs of a wrathclaw or daggertooth.

Mally held up a limp water pouch. "Did you forget to tie it closed?" She threw it at my feet, where it sagged into the sand.

"I c-can't remember," I stammered, heat flooding my face. That had been my last water pouch.

"How could you be so stupid, Amaya?" Mally shouted.

Tau got to his feet and planted himself in front of me.

"I must have forgotten to close it."

171

"We have to keep going." Mally turned her back on me and set off for the trail. "I promised to help you, but I want to be back with my papa. We need to find Badeko and your brother fast."

A sudden distance opened up between us. Feeling hurt, I followed Mally along the trail.

Chapter Seventeen

"The crickets have stopped their noise"

The sun had fallen, but the air was still hot enough to make every breath feel heavy.

We ran to make up lost time, chasing the sun across the sky. Thirst started as a nagging thought but soon became all I could think about. Saliva turned into a paste in my mouth that I struggled to swallow. A headache clamped tight around my skull.

"I'm too hot." I stopped to pull off my tunic top.

"No." Mally grabbed my hand. "You need to keep the layers on; it will stop the moisture from your sweat evaporating."

I pulled my tunic down, feeling the panic-beast crawl into my chest, against my heart that beat too fast. The thirst was suffocating.

Now we plodded at walking pace, neither of us able to move any faster.

Tau sniffed at something to the side of the dusty path. *Bones.* I could make out the spiralling horns of a short-tailed buck, pointing upwards at the blue sky. The empty eye sockets watched me as I walked past, leaving me with a feeling of dread.

Time turned to treacle. *Are we almost there?* Everything looked white. Too bright.

Mally weaved along the path. I could only watch as she almost stumbled into a burrow hole, my tongue too clumsy to shout a warning.

I thought about the lake, the beautiful sparkling lake. The cold on my skin. Opening my mouth and letting the water flow in. Filling me up. Diving down into the dark part of the lake. I could almost hear the splashing, pouring, cascading water.

Where am I? For a moment I thought I could hear the croak of the spadefoots that lived in the mud. I could hear the fisherfolk chatting to each other, reeling in their lines.

But all I could see was Tau and Mally and the cracked earth path.

Mally tumbled, smacking into the dust with a thump. I staggered over to her.

"Thirsty," she muttered at me.

"You have to get up." I tried to pull her up but she wasn't budging.

I slumped down next to her. It felt good to stop walking.

"Can't move any more," she mumbled. She closed her eyes.

Maybe we can just rest for a moment. I felt so tired.

I let my eyelids shut, remembering the last time I'd seen Kaleb. When he'd fallen asleep in my arms, next to the hearth. *Close your eyes and breathe in deep.*

Clods of dirt landed on my lap. I opened my eyes to see Tau digging in the ground. *What's he doing?* I wondered without much curiosity. Everything felt like a dream.

Tau grunted as he strained against something in the ground, and his teeth clamped on to whatever it was. With a jerk of his head, the something came loose and he dragged it over to me.

It looked like a huge plant root, pale white with wormlike tubers extending out of it.

The root felt spongy as I wiped the dirt off it.

What is it?

Mally opened her eyes. Her mouth was cracked in the corners, just like I could feel mine was too.

Suddenly, she made a strange squawking sound and grabbed the root out of my hands.

I tried to grab it back off her, but she batted my hand away.

"It's an alka-root!" She fumbled for her knife and unsheathed it.

"What are you doing?" I felt a rush of alarm at the sight of the sharp blade.

Mally stabbed the root, up to the hilt.

Liquid dribbled out.

Feeling dazed, I watched Mally put her lips to the cut and slurp noisily. As if noticing me for the first time, she made another incision.

"Drink!" She handed me the root.

I copied what she'd done. The salty-sweet liquid poured into my mouth, soothing my painful and swollen tongue and swilling down my parched throat.

It was the most beautiful thing I'd ever tasted.

We drank from the root, squeezing the plant between our hands and channelling the water down our thumbs to capture the moisture in our mouths.

I would have cried if my dry eyes had let me.

Mally let out a burst of laughter. "Your goat is pretty useful."

"His name's Tau." I hugged him so tight he wriggled out of my embrace.

Mally stood up and pulled me on to my feet, both of us feeling wobbly.

"You ready to carry on?" Mally looked concerned. "Or should we rest for a bit in the shade?"

"We don't really have much choice. It's going to start getting dark soon." Now that I felt more alert, I noticed the softening of the sky, the blue turning into pink.

Besides, the water from the plant had given me back some strength. Enough to get us to the refuge hut, I hoped.

We walked along, squishing the last moisture out of the root into our mouths, and as the sun travelled further west, the air cooled. We kept quiet to save energy.

With the temperature drop, the crickets started their evening noise. The high-pitched hum set my nerves on edge. I could feel the moon behind us, waiting below the horizon. The Switching Hour was close.

Mally pulled the map out of her pack and studied it as we walked.

"We're near to the refuge hut," she murmured. Her cheeks were flushed, her eyes too bright. She didn't look well. Spending so much time exposed to the sun had done her more harm than it had to me. Tau ran ahead, close enough that I could hear the patter of his hooves on the hardpacked ground.

I stopped and grabbed hold of Mally's arm. She winced at the pressure of my fingers.

"What's wrong?" she said.

"The crickets have stopped their noise."

The long grass was eerily silent. I unhooked the latch that kept my axe secure and clutched the handle tightly.

Nothing made a sound.

I started walking again, but Mally grabbed my arm and pulled me back to a stop.

She held her finger to her lips and motioned for me to listen.

"We need to go!" I whispered fiercely.

Mally cocked her head to one side. "I heard something," she said.

Then I heard it too.

The small sound of a baby crying.

It came from further into the forest, the dark space in the middle of a thicket of needle-thorn trees.

"It's a baby!" Mally tightened her grip on my arm, pinching my skin.

My heart fluttered like a trapped bird in a cage. I knew that sound.

I tried to pull her away. "No, it's not. It's another trick. We need to get to the refuge before the Switching Hour begins!"

The baby cried louder. It sounded closer this time, just out of sight.

Mally planted her feet against my pulling. Tau bleated. His ears twitched this way and that. I put a hand on his back to try and calm him.

"Mally, you have to trust me. I've heard it before! Badeko can mimic the sound of a baby crying, but it's not real. We have to leave now!" The dark was seeping into the light, the sun was beginning to set.

"Badeko takes people away, doesn't it?" I couldn't tell if she was talking to me. Her foot swished the grass that lined the dirt path.

"What are you doing, Mally!" I clamped my fingers around her arm.

The cry sounded once more.

The noise was so familiar. It didn't sound like a baby any more. It sounded like a toddling, a bawling sound that filled my head.

"It's not real," I whispered, but I heard the flicker of doubt in my words.

I've heard it before! My breath caught in my throat. It was the sound that Kaleb made when I threw MeeMa, his rag doll, into the fire. I remembered the sting of hurt in his voice.

"Kaleb," I whispered. My fingers loosened their grip. Mally shrugged me away and stepped off the path.

I snatched for her sleeve but it was too late. She disappeared between the trees.

The crying stopped. The crickets resumed their chirruping as if they'd never paused.

"Mally!" I shouted after her. "If I go into the forest, then we'll both be lost!" I stared at Tau as if he had the answer, but he just watched me with his brown eyes. He trembled but didn't bolt.

"Mally!" I called again at the space where she had disappeared. But she didn't answer. "Come on, Tau. We have to find her."

We stepped off the trail and towards the thicket of trees.

Chapter Eighteen

"I can make it go back to the way it was"

Long grass swished against my legs. I stomped my feet to scare any hiding snakes.

Tau ploughed through the grass at my side, his horned head just above it. We reached the needle-thorn trees and I ducked low to avoid the spikes on the twisted branches.

"Mally?" I whispered. Something made me feel like I needed to keep my voice down. There was the prickle of watching eyes.

The branches of the trees snaked across the sky, a blaze of orange and red.

I grasped Tau's collar and held on tight. "Keep your eyes open, Tau. Don't let anything sneak up on us!" I whispered. Tau grunted back.

"Mally!" I hissed. "Where are you?" Brushing hair

away from my ears, I heard nothing apart from the unceasing cricket drone.

Then I caught a snatch of her green dress in the dark. She was standing between two needle-thorn trees, her back towards me.

"Mally?" I stepped forward cautiously. She seemed fixated on something I couldn't see.

I stopped behind her, an arm's length away, and when I saw what she was staring at I gasped.

A man stood a few paces in front of Mally. He looked like her, with his wide apart eyes and sharp jawline. He had a ragged beard and hair that stuck out in all directions. I had a flash of recognition but couldn't anchor it. He made no indication he could see me or Tau, or even Mally. The blurry outline of another person stood next to him, as if it was his shadow.

In his arms he held a baby and it started to cry.

Mally trembled. "I can make it go back to the way it was," she whispered.

She stepped towards him, as if in a trance.

"No!" I lunged forward and grabbed her arm. She spun to face me.

"I don't want to hurt it!" she sobbed. Tears dripped off her jaw. "I just want everything to go back to the way it was!"

I pulled her away from the thing that wasn't her papa.

"We have to go!" I grabbed a handful of her sleeve and pulled her forward, only letting go when I knew she would follow.

We wove our way back towards the trail.

"It's not far," I said, without knowing if it was true or not.

Tau stopped so suddenly, I bumped into him. I gave him a shove, but he planted his feet.

"Move, Tau!"

I felt eyes prickle along my skin, making my hairs stand up. The heat from being watched. Then I saw them. The markings were unmistakable.

"Don't move, Mally," I whispered. I heard the intake of her breath, as she saw them too.

The daggertooths were back.

They had us surrounded, a whole pack of them. The white patterns on their backs blending into the yellow grass. They were wary of us, only the boldest coming close.

The largest daggertooth moved forward. The blades of its shoulders rolled as it lowered itself closer to the ground.

"What are we going to do?" Mally hissed. Her

breath tickled my ear, as she tried to make herself seem smaller than me. Realizing she was using me as a human shield, I elbowed her sharply in the ribs.

The rest of the pack skittered between the trees, darting behind cover but always there, waiting. The large daggertooth crept even nearer, so close I could see the grey hairs around its muzzle and the gold glint in its eyes.

A pause, where the breath caught in my throat, then the daggertooth leaped. I flung my arms around my head, squeezing my eyes tight shut.

No impact, only a *thump* and a yelp.

I peeked out between my arms and saw Tau. He had jumped between me and the daggertooth and knocked it back with his horns. The daggertooth sprawled in the dust, before twisting itself upright again and backing away with a low growl.

A sudden cold at my back and I realized Mally was no longer there. I spun around, catching sight of her green dress as she dashed away into the grass.

She's abandoned us!

Three daggertooths slunk away from the watching pack and followed her, padding on light feet. I wanted to shout a warning but it was too late; she had disappeared between the trees.

The large daggertooth had shaken off Tau's rebuttal. It darted forward, nipping at Tau's feet, but Tau was ready. He threw himself into the attack, strong horns against snapping teeth.

The rest of the pack were holding back; I counted six of them. Some old and sick, with hunger sharpening their ribs. Others too young to fight; fear and inexperience flattened their ears and left them cowering.

Feeling sick at leaving him, I turned away from Tau and ran through the trees. I hated Mally for making me desert Tau. For only thinking of herself. But I couldn't leave her to the jackals, even if she could do it to me.

The moon had risen and filtered through the trees so I could see more clearly now. I found her only paces away, standing still as if she was a tree herself. Her wide eyes told me to stop.

No yipping noise or even a scrunch of dirt shifting beneath their paws. They moved like ghosts, flitting around Mally in closing circles. One would dart forward, before reeling back, only for another to take its place. So skinny and light, they looked harmless. But when hunger steals away fear, any creature with sharp enough teeth can kill.

I slowly bent down and felt around for a stone or rock.

A branch. I grasped it tight, relieved at how heavy and solid it felt.

I caught Mally's eye. She took a step towards me.

"No, Mally!" My warning came too late.

Quick as a snake bite, a daggertooth nipped her arm, tearing her sleeve.

Mally screamed.

The daggertooth darted away, its sharp eyes locked on her.

Bolder now, the other two sprinted forward and yanked at the hem of her dress.

Mally was flung to the ground and her head smacked into the hard dirt. Her breath came out in one sharp gasp of pain.

The daggertooths dragged her further into the trees, her body limp. Another daggertooth danced around her, looking for the moment to strike.

I got there first.

Swinging the branch upwards, I knocked a blow into the daggertooth's side, sending it yelping into the trees. The other two jackals flinched away from another swing of my branch. They let go of Mally's dress, but didn't go far – I could still see their glassy eyes above the grass. Waiting for me to turn my back.

Something rustled to the left, through the long grass. *The rest of the pack!*

I held the branch up high, ready to crack it downwards.

Tau trotted towards us, his chest heaving and his breath snorting in and out.

I dropped the branch and called him over. He flinched when I tried to pull him closer, and I could see there was a deep cut on his nose.

"You're bleeding," I whispered.

Mally.

She was still on the ground. Her breathing was shallow; I could only hear it with my own breath held in. I moved her hair away from her face. Warm, sticky blood had oozed into the knots, clumping it together. There was a deep cut above her eyebrow, clotted with dirt.

She groaned.

I helped her to stand, glancing around for a sign of the daggertooths. I couldn't see them any more, but I could *feel* them. They hadn't left us yet.

"Climb up." I patted Tau's broad back. He waited patiently as Mally clambered on and held on tight.

She snatched out her hand and grabbed my shoulder, forcing me to turn around.

"I'm sorry," she hissed through teeth clenched in pain. "For everything."

I shrugged off her hand and her apology. Her actions had put Tau's life at risk. And mine. *And Kaleb's.*

I patted Tau's chest and he stamped his hoof as if to say he was ready.

We edged away. *Where was Badeko now?*

As if on cue, there was the shrill sound of a crying baby. This time it was a threat, not a lure. A cacophony of crying, wailing and screaming. Baby sounds, toddling voices and unintelligible gibberish distorted the air.

Badeko's mocking us!

"Hang on!" I told Mally.

The baby cries were louder now. The air was full of the sound of them.

I grabbed hold of Tau's collar and shouted, "Run!"

Chapter Nineteen

"I don't know which way to go!"

Tau weaved through the trees, ducking his curved horns out of the way of the branches. Mally hung on, her arms locked around his neck. My eyes strained to catch the last of the daylight – I could barely see a few paces in front of us.

I stumbled and fell heavily, knocking the wind from my lungs. Tau stopped until I could grasp on to his collar, and find my feet before setting off again.

We emerged panting on to the path. In the gloom, the dirt track looked like a black river, slicing through the trees on either side. I peered towards the horizon, where the sun was half set.

"The Switching Hour is almost over!" I said. "Come on, Tau!"

I pulled on Tau's collar to get him moving again,

but I didn't know which way to run. The needle-thorn trees and the long grass were a tangle of shapes and shadows.

"I don't know which way to go!"

But Tau knew. He pulled away to the left with Mally still clinging on to his back. *I have to trust him!* I ran alongside and strained to listen for any sign of the daggertooths or Badeko above the thud of my feet and Tau's hooves against the ground.

And there it was. *The refuge hut.* Relief flooded through me.

We reached it and Tau headbutted the door open with his horns. I helped Mally slide off his back then followed them both inside and locked the door behind us.

"We're safe." I breathed through my nose, to slow my heartbeat.

Mally's stifled sobs filled the quiet of the room. Tau snuffled my hand and I wrapped my arm around his neck, pulling him close.

"Mally, can you make a fire?" I needed to see how badly Tau was hurt. I pressed my face against his neck and my tears soaked into his coat.

Mally shuffled around the fireplace. I heard her stacking wood and the rustle of dry leaves and kindling. I cradled Tau's head. His breath came out in warm puffs against my arm. Too fast and shallow.

"It's OK," I whispered into his ear. "We're safe now."

A spark from Mally's flint and the dry leaves she'd piled in the hearth caught alight. She added twigs and the fire grew big enough for us to see the small room. Like the other huts, the floor was beaten earth and the only furniture was two small beds, a table and some cooking utensils.

I led Tau closer to the firelight and inspected him for injury. The cut on his nose oozed blood; it dripped on to my hand. I wiped it off on my tunic.

"Mally, do you have anything to help the wound heal?"

Mally had stood back, her hands around her face, as if she was too scared to look.

"Is he OK?" she choked.

"He'll be fine."

Mally burst into fresh sobs, her whole body shaking.

"Mally!" I barked at her. "You have to help me!"

She ran to her pack and began taking out jars. I recognized the green leaves of the aloe plant in one of them.

Turning back to Tau, I carefully wiped the cut on his nose with a washcloth. We didn't have any water, so I spat on the cloth to dampen it.

Mally brought over a yellow mash and held it out to me.

"It'll help with the healing." Her eyes were red.

Tau tried to lick the mash off, even as I applied it to the cut.

"Greedy goat." I kissed his nose.

He settled down next to me, curling up and falling into a sleep. It had been a long day for all of us.

I reached towards the fire's heat, when my bracelet slipped over my wrist and dropped into the embers. I grabbed the fire tongs and rescued it, slipping it back on to my wrist in relief, and tying it tighter than before.

I dusted off the ash from the wool that was dyed blue, green and black. *The colours of the sky, the grasslands, and black for the forest.* On closer inspection, I saw there was also red wool, binding the end of the bracelet together. *What does the red wool mean?*

Granny Uma must have mended it for me at some point.

Mally slumped back down next to me, wrapping her arms around her knees.

"Why did you save me?" Her voice was strained and she didn't look at me. "Tau could have died."

I picked at the woollen threads of my bracelet, worrying the knot. I could lie and say it was because I needed her to show me the way to the Dead Tree. But I had never been very good at lying.

"Because you're my friend." I felt closer to Mally from the past few days than I had to anyone since Mama had left.

"I've been horrible to you." Mally pressed her head into her knees, muffling her words.

"Whether you're being horrible or not, we're stuck with each other now," I said. *Like family.*

Mally wiped her face on her sleeve. "Thank you," she snuffled, finally looking at me through her tangled and blood-encrusted hair.

Something still bothered me though.

"What did you mean, about wanting things to go back to the way they were?" I asked.

Mally flinched. "Nothing."

I persisted. "You went all funny, when you heard the baby crying." I remembered Mally's face when she left the path. She was scared. "And your papa was holding a baby."

A sickening thought occurred to me.

"Mally." I spoke softly. "Has Badeko taken someone from you too?" I hoped it wasn't true and was relieved when Mally shook her head.

"Then what is it?"

To my horror, she whispered, "I *wanted* it to take someone away."

It took a moment for her words to make sense to me. "Mally ... who could you possibly hate so much that you want Badeko to take them? How could you *want* that creature to steal anyone away for ever?"

"I've changed my mind, Amaya! I'm sorry I ever thought it!" she wailed.

"Who?" I shouted. "Who did you want it to take?"

Her reply was interrupted by a knock on the door. We both jumped.

"Was that a knock?" Mally's voice was shrill.

Bang! Bang! Bang!

I jumped to my feet. "Who's there?" I squeaked, wishing my voice was stronger.

"Let me in!" said a voice that was completely familiar.

"Mama?" I whispered.

Bang! Bang! Bang!

"Let me in, child!" said the voice, and right then I

knew exactly who it was.

But I wasn't going to be tricked. Not this time.

"What's my favourite food?" I asked.

I heard a cackle from behind the door. "I wish it was my pumpkin stew, but I know it's honey drizzle cake. You ate too much on your last birthday and got stomach ache."

I still wasn't sure.

"I have a birthmark," I hissed through the crack in the wood. "Where is it?"

"You have a birthmark on your ankle." I could hear her smile. "A kiss from the moon."

She'd always called it that, because I'd been born in the middle of the night.

I unlocked the door in one quick motion.

Granny Uma stood silhouetted in the doorway. I didn't think, I just threw myself into her arms and she caught me without hesitation, hugging my breath away.

"Sweet child," she whispered into my hair. "Did you think I wouldn't follow you?"

"How did you get here so quickly?" I asked.

"I had help," she said, and with that she turned and whistled. Zola and Ela trotted up to the door.

"I harnessed Zola to the yam cart to come and find you. And Ela wasn't going to be left behind,"

Granny Uma said, as she ushered us back into the house, goats and all.

"I'm not leaving them at the mercy of the night," she said, when I raised my eyebrows.

Tau bucked and skipped around the older goats like a kid, even though he was as big as them now. Ela nuzzled his face and Zola playfully swung his huge horns in Tau's direction.

The small room felt happily full, like my stomach after a feast.

I pulled Mally over to Granny Uma. "This is Mally," I said.

Granny Uma looked shocked. "This is where you've been hiding?" she said. "Your papa is very worried about you!" She waggled her finger at Mally, who looked down at her feet. "First the struggle with the baby and then you disappear. Poor man!"

Mally stuttered. "The baby ... is it..."

"*She* is fine." Granny Uma smiled. "And she can't wait to meet her big sister."

Mally burst into tears. Granny Uma walked over to her and put her arms around her, making soothing noises.

"What's going on?" I asked.

Granny Uma let go of Mally and said, "You

haven't told Amaya?"

Once again, Mally wouldn't catch my eye. "My papa and step-mama, they were having a baby." She tried to keep the hurt out of her voice but I could read it there.

"You left because your papa was having another child?"

Mally untucked her hair from behind her ear. "I was afraid I wasn't wanted any more."

I put everything together in my head. "You wanted Badeko to take your new sister away. Is that right?"

"I don't want that any more," Mally said quickly, glancing at Granny Uma.

Granny Uma laughed. "Badeko isn't going to take her away." She smoothed Mally's hair away from her face. "I helped deliver the baby and she is beautiful. Just like her sister." She wiped Mally's tears with her thumb. "But your papa is very worried. He left for the Forest Settlement to find you the minute he realized you were missing."

My mind was spinning. "The man who came to ask for Granny Uma's help." I remembered the red-haired man who had arrived at our cottage in a panic. "That's your father?"

Granny Uma nodded. "Luca and Sadi will both be relieved that I've found their runaway daughter." She tapped her finger against her temple. "Lucky for you both I have a map of the forest up here," she said. "When I read your note, Amaya, I knew you would keep to the woodcutters' track and find refuge in the huts at night, if you had any sense."

I turned to Mally. "So your papa didn't read your note?"

"I didn't leave a note," she whispered. "I didn't want him to find me."

"He has no idea where you are?" I gasped.

Granny Uma held her hands up, palms facing us both. "You are safe, that's all that matters right now. We'll get you back to your papa, Mally, don't you worry."

She pointed to the packs she'd brought with her. "There's food in each; I'm sure you're both hungry. We'll make something to eat before we sleep."

Mally grabbed a water pouch and threw another one at me. I drank enough to slake my thirst, before letting Tau drink from my hand.

Despite complaining of the lack of a stove, Granny Uma conjured up a stew and soon had us seated around the table and sharing out hunks of hearth-warmed bread with curls of melting butter and pickled sunfruit. Tau and the other goats had been given their mash and they'd curled up next to each other. Tau seemed happy to be back with them.

"I'm glad I've found you, girls." Granny Uma cut another slice of bread and slid it on to my plate. "Ten families have now been inflicted by the Sorrow Sickness, which would account for at least ten missing children. Those who have it in the Eastern Town are in mourning, some wail without ceasing, others shut themselves away. All without knowing who they've lost."

"That's awful," Mally whispered.

I thought of the couple in the Forest Settlement, Sara and Peter, still waiting for their child to come home.

"We need to get out of the forest as soon as we can," said Granny Uma. "We'll make an early start tomorrow so that we can cover ground before the sun gets too strong." She wiped the pickle from her plate with the bread before eating it. "We'll fill the water pouches from the well for the journey home."

Mally nodded. "The last refuge's well was drying up; we can't count on it to have water when we get back there."

I watched them both. Something wasn't right. "We're going home?" I said.

"Of course!" Granny Uma said. "The sooner we get Mally back to her family the better."

I struggled to remember. It was like trying to breathe underwater. "But what about Kaleb? We need to rescue him!" I said.

Granny Uma narrowed her eyes. "Who?"

"Kaleb," I repeated, and my chest squeezed when Granny Uma's face didn't change. "My brother!"

Granny Uma looked confused. "But, Amaya," she said slowly, as my heart began to race. "You don't have a brother."

Chapter Twenty

"You were there!"

I felt cold all over, from the inside out. "Kaleb," I whispered. "His name is *Kaleb*."

But even as I said it, the doubt crept into my voice. I couldn't keep the memories from escaping: there were too many holes.

Granny Uma laid a gentle hand on my arm but I pulled away.

"No!" I shouted. "You have to remember him!" I stood up, making Mally wince as the chair scraped across the floor with a shriek.

"Amaya, I came to find you," Granny Uma said. "I read your note, that you were headed for the Forest Settlement." The crags in her face were shadowed by tiredness. It was a face that was so familiar, her dark eyes were Mama's and mine. Her skin the same shade of the earth. *Could it be that it was only ever Granny Uma, Mama and me?*

No. There was someone else as well. Someone younger than me.

Kaleb. I stored the name away, placing it with the memories of Mama. Hiding it from the empty space, the darkness that threatened to take them both away from me.

"Mally, you must remember me speaking of my brother? He's the reason we have to find Badeko," I implored her. She pushed her empty plate away, her brow furrowed in thought. She slowly shook her head.

"You never mentioned having a brother," she said. "We were going to ask Badeko to take away my new baby sister, don't you remember?" Mally shifted uncomfortably in her seat, avoiding Granny Uma's disapproving stare.

I remembered what Mally had said. That she wouldn't be able to hold on to the memory of Kaleb, not while Badeko had him and was eating his dreams.

She's not going to be any help.

I turned to Granny Uma. "You were there!" I cried. "You helped Mama give birth to him. I remember you being there!" I was crumbling, piece by piece.

"But, Amaya..." Granny Uma reached out across the table towards me. "Surely I would remember looking after two children!" She tried to catch my hand in hers. "Your mama only ever had one child."

"No!" I shouted. "Badeko has taken him!"

Granny Uma picked at the clatterpod seeds strung up on her necklace, her mouth a taut line.

Tears of frustration prickled my eyes as I tried to keep myself from falling apart.

"Are you sure you're not suffering from the heat?" Granny Uma spoke softly, as if I was ill. "You've been out in the sun for several days."

"No." I clenched my hands in my lap. "The creature has taken Kaleb."

There was still no flicker of recollection at his name on Granny Uma's face.

"There is nothing we can do tonight," she finally said. "But if you are certain, then we will look for him tomorrow. We will see."

I didn't resist when she wrapped a wool blanket around me. It smelled of hay and dried jasmine flowers and pumpkin skins.

Trembling, I curled up on the floor with Tau by

my side. I listened to the thud of his heart until it became a soothing song that calmed my shaking bones.

Soon, Granny Uma's snoring and Mally's deep breathing filled the room.

Sitting up, I reached for the stone the colour of my mama's eyes, before remembering I'd lost it, the pain hitting me anew.

I studied the inside of my pocket as if I could make it reappear, but all that was there was charcoal dust.

Tau raised his head and looked towards the door.

"Did you hear something?" I breathed into his ear, so as not to wake the others.

Slowly, I got up and stealthily moved towards the door. Tau grunted a warning.

Crouching down on my hands and knees, I peeked under the door.

At first, I couldn't see anything. Then something moved in the darkness. I squinted and focused on the space, between the two posts that held up the porch roof.

Someone walked away from the door. Two small bare feet, covered in mud.

I jumped up and ran over to the window.

Splinters from the rough wood shutters dug into my cheek, but I could peer out enough to see the person outside. A small boy, his back towards the house. My heart hammered against my throat. *Kaleb.*

I knew it wasn't really Kaleb. It was Badeko. The Dream Eater making me see things that weren't real. It was trying to bring me outside using the one thing I wanted most in the world.

But if the *thing* outside, the Dream Eater's vison of Kaleb, could turn around, then I would be able to see his face. I would remember what my brother looked like.

"I could make the empty space disappear," I whispered, my breath visible on the glass.

But the small boy kept walking, stepping off the porch and on to the dry grass that looked silver from the light of the moon and stars.

In two steps, I was back at the door and I eased the bolt across.

Tau was by my side in a second, tugging on my tunic with his teeth.

"I'll be careful!" I hissed, pushing his horned head away.

I cracked the door open and stepped into the night, Tau still latched on to my tunic.

The thing that looked like my brother was already halfway across the clearing. He would soon reach the trees and disappear into the darkness.

I stepped off the porch.

"Wait!" I called out.

He stopped. The night air was stiflingly close and heavy. The moonlight picked out the small curls on his head, stirring in an imaginary breeze.

"Kaleb?" I stepped closer. The hard ground was cold, the heat had escaped with the sun.

The toddling half-turned, as if he could hear my voice but was unsure where it was coming from. His yellow shirt looked grubby and wrinkled. I resisted the sharp urge to run to him.

I could almost see the small boy's face, when my ears picked up a sound. A song without words. Each note felt like honey, sticky and warm. It clung to my skin and oozed into my ears.

"Please, Kaleb," I pleaded. "Look at me!"

He turned around; I finally saw him.

But there was nothing there.

Where his face should have been, there was just a darkness as empty as my memory was. A blur that I couldn't focus on. My stomach flipped as the ground shifted.

The empty space has taken him from me. Without his face, who am I looking for?

A hunger grew in my stomach, knotting my belly into painful twists. The hairs on my arm stood up as the humming reverberated against my skin. A song like distant thunder, drowning out the cricket noise.

I tried to turn away, but my feet were glued to the earth. I couldn't move.

The song filled my lungs like smoke. I tried to claw at my throat, but I couldn't feel my fingers or my toes. My arms were too heavy.

Breathe. I focused on the rise and fall of my chest. Air in and air out.

The boy without a face was changing shape. More legs, more arms, grew from his elongating body. Two milk-white eyes appeared in the empty space.

Something shimmered silver-grey in the white of the moon: a net spread between Badeko's twitching arms.

A dagger-sharp pain in my toes brought me painfully awake. The pain zigzagged lightning-fast up my whole body and the song faltered.

I looked down. Tau was standing with all his weight on my foot, his sharp hooves almost cracking my toes. I'd forgotten he was there.

Hobbling backwards, I grabbed hold of Tau's collar with both hands.

"Quick, Tau!" I gasped. He pulled me towards the house.

I glanced over my shoulder, searching for Badeko, but the clearing was empty.

It was like it had all been a bad dream. A nightmare.

We made it to the porch and I stumbled through the door, Tau still leading me.

I slammed the lock back into place and slumped to the floor, clutching my sore foot. Tau nuzzled my hair apologetically.

"What are you doing, child?" Granny Uma shuffled over, a blanket wrapped around her shoulders. "Are you hurt?"

"I'm fine, Granny Uma. I stubbed my toe while checking the door was locked."

I couldn't erase the image of the empty face: the terrible blur that had threatened to suck me in.

I hobbled to the bed, supported by Granny Uma and Tau. I collapsed on to the blanket that smelled of wool-moth's wings.

"Can you sing me the rhyme, Granny Uma?" I asked.

"Which rhyme, Amaya?"

"The bedtime rhyme that Mama used to sing." I was so tired, but I needed to hear it. "The one you used to sing to her, before sleep."

"I remember it," Granny Uma said softly, brushing the curls away from my damp forehead.

> *Close your eyes and breathe in deep*
> *It's time for you to go to sleep*
> *Until the moon has gone to hide*
> *I will be right by your side.*

I thought of Kaleb, sleeping alone in the Dead Tree's hollow.

I must remember. I will not forget.

The creature crept up the side of the Dead Tree, its many legs catching on to the cracks in the bark. It gnashed its teeth in anger.

It scuttled into the hollow, scuffing the dead leaves to the side. Tonight, it would have the last meal from the boy, whose dreams were only wisps now. It wasn't enough to ease the hunger that was growing in its belly. It needed more.

But for now, it would savour the last slurps of

sweet dreams, that tasted of wet earth, goats' milk and something else. If the creature knew what love was, that's what the boy's dreams were full of. Warm heart and fierce strength.

Chapter Twenty One

"You woke up screaming"

Agonizing pain tore me away from sleep. I cried out and clutched my forehead, but I couldn't make it stop.

It was pain with jagged edges and tearing teeth. Pain that burrowed deep into my brain. It expanded outwards, pressing against the backs of my eyes. I shut them tight, but lightning flashed and sparked against my eyelids like a storm was raging inside my skull.

I shivered. I could feel every nerve in my body as if a swarm of ants were scuttling over my skin. Bile whooshed upwards from the pit of my stomach. I retched over the side of the bed, but only water came up.

I wrapped my arms around my head, but the

pain was trapped inside and growing bigger. I heard the howl of a toddling, then realized the noise was coming from me.

I heard a small and distant voice say, "Drink!" I felt a cool hand on my arm. Someone lifted my head up and poured liquid into my mouth. I choked, but some went down my scraped-raw throat. A damp cloth was placed on my forehead; the water dripped and soaked into my hair.

The white flashes against my eyelids slowly flickered. The storm inside my head began to dissolve and the iron clamp around my head eased as the pain let go.

I opened my eyes.

Mally was staring at me. She had a wooden cup in her hand, and she placed it on the floor. She took the wet cloth from my forehead.

I groaned. My whole body ached.

"You woke up screaming," Mally said. She watched me closely, concern furrowed into her brow.

I tried to sit up but my arms crumpled and I fell on to the blanket. "The pain. It was tearing my head apart," I managed to whisper, but every word boomed too loud in my ears.

Mally brushed the damp hair away from my forehead. "I gave you a drink made from the root of a pincushion tree. It dulls the pain, but you must rest," she said. "I'll make you some food."

Tau licked the water that dripped down my temples, his tongue rasping against my skin in a way that was strangely soothing. I wrapped my arms around him and pressed my forehead into his warm neck.

I peered around the room. Mally was cooking over the fire, and the smell of porridge bubbled out of the pot. The door was open and dawn light flooded into the hut.

"Where's Granny Uma?" I asked.

"She's gone to fetch some water from the well, ready for the journey home."

Now that the pain had gone, there was a nagging thought that hid just out of reach.

Granny Uma walked through the door, lugging a pail of well water. "You're awake, sleep-snatcher!" She beamed at me. "Let's not waste the daylight hours; it's time we made our way home."

Slowly, I sat up, my bones aching. "I feel strange."

"You've probably got sunstroke from walking in the heat for the last few days." Granny Uma came over and placed her hand, still wet from the well, on my forehead. "You're burning up, Amaya."

Mally brought over a cup of water. Granny Uma made me drink some sips. "You need to keep hydrated," she said, smoothing a stray curl behind my ear.

Handing the cup back to Mally, I swung my legs out of the bed and tried to stand, but I had to lean heavily on Granny Uma as a wave of dizziness washed over me. "I don't feel right, Granny Uma."

To my surprise, I realized my foot was bruised. I couldn't remember what I'd done to it. I gingerly put weight on it and was relieved that it was only bruised, not broken.

Granny Uma looked like she hadn't slept well, and there were dark shadows under her eyes. "We need to get back to the grasslands, where we have clean water from the lake and fresh food," she said. "It's not good to be in the forest during a drought like this."

The fire hissed and spat. Mally jumped up and hoisted the pot off the fire hook, using metal tongs.

She took it over to the table and dished porridge out into three bowls. My stomach heaved with the thought of eating; I couldn't get the taste of bile out of my mouth.

"I need some air," I said, ignoring the concern that flashed across both their faces.

Leaving the table, I walked to the door. The sun had begun its journey across the sky, and slants of bright light made their way through the branches of the tall densewood trees. I walked out into the clearing where the dry grass crumbled into dust under my feet.

Mally came and stood next to me.

"How's your headache?" she asked.

"Fine," I replied. But I still didn't *feel* right. Like I was wearing clothes that were too small for me.

I watched Tau search for roots, snuffling the ground around the clearing.

Then he flicked his head and stamped his hooves in the red dust. He ran over and pushed me with his curved horns, grunting.

I pushed back. "Stop it, Tau!" I yelled at him. *Why was he acting like this?* I'd never seen him behave so aggressively towards me.

But Tau shoved me again, so forcefully I fell backwards.

I kicked out at Tau, hitting him hard on the side. "Stop it!" I exploded.

Tau watched me warily. "Go away!" I said fiercely

and waved my arms. Anger raged through my veins as fast as a forest fire. I couldn't control it. *Something* wasn't right.

Tau turned and bounded away down the trail. But not the trail homewards. The one that led to the forest's centre.

I jumped up; all my anger turned to fright. I chased after him, but he had fled.

"Tau!" I shouted, scaring a flock of weaving birds out of their nests. I listened over the whir of their wings but I couldn't hear him. I ran further into the forest, losing sight of the cottage behind me.

"Stop, Amaya!" Mally shouted, running behind me. "You can't follow him. It's too dangerous!"

She caught my arm. I shook it off.

"I can't leave him behind," I sobbed. "He's my family!"

I wanted to run into the forest. I didn't care about the dangers. But my thoughts were a swarm of flies; I couldn't pick one from the other. I didn't trust myself to think straight.

"Let's tell Granny Uma," Mally said, pulling me back towards the cottage. "She'll know what to do."

*

Granny Uma had packed our things and loaded them on to the cart. Zola was harnessed to it, with Ela by his side.

"Let's go home." Granny Uma looked around. "Where's Tau?"

"He ran into the forest." Mally pointed to the densewood trees. "Shall we go after him?"

Granny Uma sighed and shook her head. "He will follow us. We don't want to waste precious time heading further away from home," she said.

Granny Uma clicked her tongue at Zola and he started walking. Ela followed by his side.

Mally put her arm around my shoulder. "I'm sure Tau will follow. He's a clever goat, he will find us." She squeezed my shoulder. But I didn't feel better. I was leaving him behind.

Feeling dazed, I followed the others along the path that led back towards the dry riverbed. Back towards home. *I should feel glad*. But my heart ached. I felt a crushing weight of sadness, clinging to me like a heavy cloak that I couldn't shake off.

There was *something* else. Something else I was leaving behind.

But I couldn't remember what it was.

To my surprise, tears rolled down my cheeks.

There was nothing I could do to stop them. It was worse than the pain that I'd felt in my head – this pain was from deep inside my chest. I tried to swallow my tears, but my throat was too tight.

I couldn't understand *why*. My mind and my body were disconnected, and I was stuck somewhere in between.

When Granny Uma had told me Mama was gone, I had cried the same tears. I had felt as though a piece of me had been taken away, like I wasn't whole.

Mally pulled me close, and I leaned against her. Her hair caught on my wet cheeks and snotty nose but I couldn't stop the sobs that quaked through my body.

I heard the harness rope thud to the ground, as Granny Uma left Zola's side and came over, putting an arm around my shoulders.

"We'll be home in a few days," she said. Her voice sounded too high. Too tight.

"Can you feel it too?" I asked her. The burning pain in my chest expanded.

Granny Uma nodded. "The Sorrow Sickness." Her body shuddered. I could feel the tremor though her arms.

"It hurts," I gasped. I couldn't breathe. My heart raced but it didn't feel like mine. *Breathe.* I focused on the rise and fall of my chest. *Air in and air out.* But it didn't work this time. My throat was too raw.

Everything started to go grey. The world began to lose its colour. Darkness crept around my peripheral vison. Shadows moved just out of sight, whichever way I looked.

What's happening? Birdsong muted. Even the ceaseless droning of the crickets hushed.

Granny Uma slumped against the cart. She muttered things under her breath, words I couldn't catch. Mally ran to Granny Uma with a shout of alarm, grabbing her arm to steady her, but I couldn't move.

A coldness travelled up my back.

I suddenly felt so alone, like I was standing on the edge of the earth, far away from anyone.

"Amaya, what's wrong?" Mally called out, not wanting to leave Granny Uma, but the shadows were creeping up behind her. They were coming for me.

"The Sorrow Sickness." I couldn't stop shaking.

A darkness, as black as the bottom of the lake, surrounded me. I felt the shadows seep under my fingernails like smoke. I pressed my hands together, but the dark was already under my skin, leeching into the marrow of my bones.

I closed my eyes tight but the darkness was replaced by flames. Fear gripped like a steel trap around my throat. I could smell burning.

Something's been taken from me. It felt like my heart had been cut out and stolen, there was only a hole where it had been. The panic-beast grew bigger, fighting to get out.

Mama.

Mama had been taken from me.

Was the Sorrow Sickness from missing Mama?

No. There was someone else.

Someone who I couldn't remember.

A muffled bleat sounded from behind us.

I opened my eyes. The darkness was still there, but I searched the path.

Tau bounded into sight. My heart pounded as relief flooded through me, shrinking the panic-beast in my stomach.

Mally gave a whoop. "You see? Tau found us!"

Tau bounded down the path and headed straight for me. I pulled him into a hug.

"Look, there's something in his mouth," Mally said.

I turned Tau to face me. A piece of cloth hung from his jaw.

"What have you got, Tau?" Mally said.

Tau dropped it on the ground at my feet.

A doll made of sackcloth.

Chapter Twenty Two

"Her name is MeeMa"

I picked it up. The doll had black woollen hair. A blue dress. Two button eyes.

I cradled the doll, but numbness was spreading through my fingers. Up my arms.

Focus. I calmed my breathing. *In, out.*

Keep the shadows at bay.

Think of Sara and Peter. Don't let the Sorrow Sickness win.

Focus on the doll.

I traced the black buttons with my finger. "The eyes are burned," I muttered. I could still see the pumpkin seeds they were made from.

The memory triggered a spark of recognition. *I remember sewing them on to the dress.* Feeling frustrated that it wasn't working the first time.

Trying again. It had meant something to someone, to have this doll. Making it for them had been important to me.

The darkness began to lift. Everything started to come back into focus.

Mally led Granny Uma over to me and Tau. It frightened me to see how unfocused Granny Uma's eyes were. My heart beat faster and I felt dizzy.

"Whose doll is it?" Mally asked, snapping me back into the moment.

I brushed her fingers over the doll's dress. Bits of scorched material fell away.

"It looks like she's been in a fight with a fire!" Mally said.

Her words ignited a memory. An image of the doll being picked out of flames. I searched through the farthest corners of my mind. I remembered being angry. Then the feeling of shame. *Had I done something terrible?*

I suddenly remembered the name of the doll.

"Her name is MeeMa." I just didn't know *how* I knew that.

The hot sun stung my shoulders. An insect crawled over my foot, tickling my toes. A fly buzzed around my head but I didn't bat it away.

I closed my eyes and shut out the world. I blocked out the sounds of the forest, the presence of Mally, Granny Uma and Tau. I squeezed my eyes tight and held the doll close to my chest.

I tried to remember where I had seen the doll before, but there was nothing. A darkness where the memory should have been. There was only empty space.

Instead of forcing myself to remember, I let my thoughts be still and quiet.

Instead of fighting it, I let the empty space surround me.

An image appeared from out of the darkness. It was as delicate as a butterfly as if one exhaled breath could scare it away. I saw flickers of blue and green. The feeling of cold water against my hot skin.

The lake! The memory brought with it a bubble of happiness. Splashed water and the sound of laughter. The excitement of knowing that I would one day pass on my knowledge of how to duck and dive for fish.

There was a presence of another person in my memory. A glimmer in the darkness.

"It was *someone* that I had been looking after," I whispered.

More memories began to appear. The feeling of a toddling child tied up with a shawl against my back. The annoyance of small grabbing fingers in my hair.

I remembered my hand, as it gently rose and fell in time with sleeping breath. The warm glow I'd felt, knowing he was safe.

My small brother.

Kaleb.

I opened my eyes. Mally watched me, her eyes narrowed with concern. Granny Uma's tired eyes were focused on my face.

Mally tilted her head to the side, and her hair tumbled over her shoulder.

"Amaya?" She shifted her pack on her shoulders. "Are you OK?"

"The empty space," I gasped. "It isn't empty!"

"What do you mean?"

"It's full of memories!" I stuttered. "How I felt when I was with him, how I wanted to protect him." I was talking too fast, but I couldn't stop. "I remembered that I loved him, even after I'd forgotten what he looked like."

"Who?"

"Kaleb!" I laughed and squeezed the doll tight. "My brother!"

Then her eyes widened, and she inhaled sharply.

"Kaleb," she repeated back to me. "I know that name."

"We were going to the Dead Tree, to find him!"

Her eyes widened as the realization dawned on her. Heat flushed her cheeks. "I remember!"

"Once I lost the memory of him, it disappeared altogether," I said. I clutched MeeMa to my chest. I felt more solid, more *real*, than I had since I'd stepped into the forest.

I searched Granny Uma's face for recognition, but her expression was blank.

"Can't you remember, Granny Uma?" I pleaded.

"It's not *possible* that I would forget," she said firmly. "How could I forget my own daughter's child?" She shook her head, but her chin wobbled.

"It was Badeko who made you forget," I said. "It's taken Kaleb."

Untying my bracelet, I folded it into Granny Uma's hand. "Remember when he used to chew on my bracelet?" I grinned. "You called him a nibbling mouse."

Granny Uma turned the bracelet over in her hands, running her finger over the threads.

"And look," I said, reaching out and rattling her

necklace. "Don't you remember how he would grab hold of your necklace and you'd have to untangle his hands from the seeds?"

Granny Uma laughed, a burst of sound.

"The little toddling!" she gasped. "He was always getting into mischief, pulling up the cabbage sprouts and tipping over the milk bucket." Relief washed over me.

"Kaleb," I said. "His name is Kaleb."

"Kaleb," Granny Uma repeated, with a tremble in her voice. "My grandson."

The confusion that had muddied up her eyes was gone. She looked like Granny Uma again.

I remembered the dream. The upside-down tree, white as bones.

"Kaleb must have dropped MeeMa along the way to the Dead Tree and somehow Tau found it." I already knew Tau had a great nose; he was able to know where to dig for roots by smell alone.

"He's a clever goat." Mally threw her arms around his neck, something she hadn't done before. Granny Uma chucked him under the chin, her way of showing gratitude.

I kissed him on the nose, careful not to hurt his healing wound.

I didn't think I could love Tau any more than I already did.

He had helped me remember my small brother.

"We have to go to the Dead Tree!" I pointed back towards the way we'd come. "Kaleb has been taken there."

Granny Uma grabbed Zola's harness, turning him around.

"We must hurry," she said. "There's no time to lose!"

The creature stirred. It opened one scaly eyelid, then the other.

It blinked against the light that filled the dark hollow. It slowly uncurled itself, disturbing the dry leaves that crackled under its belly. It sniffed.

Could it be? *the creature thought. It wasn't possible.*

But it was true.

The boy was dreaming once more.

The creature tried to slurp the dream through sharp teeth, but the dream couldn't be eaten. The dream was too alive. It fought against the song's net with the strength of a thousand fish. The net wouldn't be able to hold it for much longer.

The Fire Dreamer must be getting closer.

Chapter Twenty Three

"The rains have forgotten us"

The sun was a quarter away from the middling time.

"Will we be able to reach the tree before the Switching Hour?" I asked Mally.

"If we hurry," she said, without slowing down.

We followed the trail that led further away from home. The densewood trees were stripped of their leaves, and the grass was sparse. No crickets hummed. Not even a fly needed batting away.

We walked in a line: Granny Uma led the way with Zola and Ela, then Mally. I followed close behind her, with Tau bumping occasionally into the back of my legs.

"Is there somewhere we can get water from, and something to eat?" Mally gasped.

Granny Uma nodded. "We will get to the

watering hole soon. I have been there before, looking for plants for medicine."

The heat of the sun grew stronger with every step, beating down on us until my head throbbed. The air grew thick, and every breath felt hot enough to scald my tongue. I wrapped my cotton scarf around my mouth to keep out the dust that kicked up with our footsteps, but still I could taste the dirt that caked my throat and rattled my lungs. The trees rippled in the heat haze.

I'd been walking in a daze, daydreaming of the grasslands, the lake and Kaleb safe at home when Granny Uma stopped abruptly, and I bumped into Mally.

"There it is!" Granny Uma pointed towards a cluster of trees. "We can stop here and wait out the middling of the day."

I shaded my eyes from the sun and saw palm trees in the distance. They shimmered in the heat, looking like waving fronds, even though the air was still. As we got closer, I could see that most of the leaves had turned brown and dropped on to the ground like broken boats.

Granny Uma led Zola and Ela into the shade of the trees, before pouring some water and grain into two small tin bowls. She patted their backs, raising red dust clouds, and murmured quietly to them.

Further away, I spotted the deep brown trunks of marago trees. My mouth watered.

I ran over, ready to climb up and pluck the fruit, but when we reached them, nothing grew on their branches. The dark green leaves had turned red with dust.

Dust. Everything is turning to dust! I slumped to the ground against the trunk of a tree. I pressed my cracked lips together and tried to swallow, but my mouth was dry. I unhooked my water pouch and untied it, wanting to pour the water down my thirsty throat but forcing myself to take sips. I spread the water over my tongue, trying to trick my mouth into thinking I wasn't thirsty any more.

The pouch felt frighteningly light. I was worried about Tau; there had been no green grass for him to eat. He nuzzled my pack, looking for food.

"Here." I poured some water into the cup of my palm, and he slurped it up, licking my hand dry. I patted some of the dust off his back, but it made me cough.

I searched for Mally and Granny Uma. They were standing under a palm tree, looking down at the ground. Granny Uma shook her head. I dropped my pack on the ground and went to join them.

"Careful." Mally put out her hand to stop me. I gasped. The ground dropped away into a ditch. At the bottom were small stones and boulders. My mind was too slow; I couldn't understand what it was.

"The watering hole. It's empty." The tearing in Mally's voice filled in the gaps between the words. "The rains have forgotten us."

I stared at the blank sky. There was nothing to suggest that the rains would appear. No thunder rumbled in the distance.

There was only the sun. Unwavering, it stared down at the world, beating on it with its hammering heat. Even when I closed my eyes, I could see the red sun through my eyelids. There was no escaping it.

I glanced back down at the dry bedrock. "There's still time!" I tried to sound confident. I forced a smile, but my dry lips split and stung. I sucked on my lip and tasted blood.

"It's never been this bad before. The rains have always arrived by now," Mally said weakly. Her face was streaked with dust that clung to her sweat. It caked in the corners of her mouth.

"Let's go back into the shade and wait for the sun

to pass overhead," I said. I guided Mally over to the marago tree.

We shared out the bread, cheese and water from the pouches. I gave Tau some of my food. I would rather we were both half hungry than Tau go without.

We sat quietly and I thought of Kaleb. Since the memory of him had reappeared, it was as if I had never forgotten. There were no frightening shadows muddling up his face or his voice. I took MeeMa out of my pack and held her in my hands. I tried to polish off the burned edges on her pumpkin seed eyes with the edge of my tunic, but they stayed black. *What is done is done.*

I hated that I'd made Kaleb cry and that it was one of the last memories he had of me.

I tucked MeeMa into my belt.

Granny Uma glanced up at the sky. "The sun is past the middling point. We can continue. We're not far now."

I fell into step beside Granny Uma, as she led Zola back on to the path.

The temperature lessened as the day went on. As the sun began to fall and the shadows lengthened, the cloudless sky let the heat escape in waves, leaving behind a chill in the air.

We ran in a line, like scurrying ants. Our footfalls fell into a rhythm, with every step bringing us closer to nightfall.

The weaving birds flew like yellow-feathered arrows back to their nests. The sun was falling down towards the horizon.

Please give us more time! I silently begged. But the sun didn't care for my small brother or me.

When the sky became tainted with the pink and purple colours of sunset, the trees thinned until there were only brittle shrubs that crunched under our feet.

"Where are we?" I searched the barren space. Then I saw it.

The white tree stood in the middle of a clearing. Its trunk was so wide, you could fit the whole of Granny Uma's cottage into the space. Its wrinkled bark was folded over itself with age, like elephant skin bleached white by the sun. Its gnarled branches only grew from the very top of the trunk, looking like roots extending into the sky.

The tree stood alone. The forest grew in a huge circle around it, as though the other trees didn't dare put down their roots too near it.

"The Dead Tree." My heart thudded in my chest. "Kaleb must be there!"

We set off across the dusty ground, leaving footprints and hoofprints in the soil behind us.

The air was much cooler now. The chill slithered over my skin, and I shivered.

The Dead Tree grew larger with each step until I had to twist my neck to see the top of it. My eyes sought out movement, but the branches were empty. Although I couldn't see a creature with milky eyes, my shoulder blades twitched with the sense of being watched.

Tau huddled next to my side. I brushed my fingers along his back. The touch of his rough fur was comforting and it gave me the courage to walk the last few steps.

"What now?" Mally whispered. Her voice still felt too loud. The hush that surrounded us was all-consuming. Even a breath felt like a ringing bell.

"I'll have to make it into the hollow," I said, looking up at the smooth, white surface of the tree.

Badeko hissed. The Old Woman, the Fire Dreamer and the Lonely One were here. It could taste the daydream smell of them, the flavour of courage and the scent of fear.

It was a delicious mix. The creature flexed its many legs, feeling the strength of the boy's dreams seep into its body.

It shivered and licked its lips. The hunger in its belly roared.

If it could ensnare the Fire Dreamer and eat her nightmares whole, the creature would be all-powerful. Animal, bird and human would fall under the Song of Sleep's spell and feed the Dream Eater's eternal hunger.

The creature would rule the night-time world.

Quickly, with its many legs, Badeko began to weave another song-net.

Granny Uma parked Zola and the cart to the side of the tree. "Stay here, Zola," she said to the billy goat, patting him on his huge head. Ela stayed next to her mate. Tau, however, stuck to my side like my shadow.

We crept around the trunk of the tree. I kept my eyes upwards, searching for the hollow. We were near the far side when I spotted it.

The opening was cave-like. As wide as I was tall, it was too high to reach.

Mally unhooked her axe from her belt and she balanced it in her hands. The last slice of sunlight caught the blade, highlighting its sharp edge. Mally grinned at me. "I'm ready," she said.

"I'll go into the hollow and get Kaleb," I said.

Granny Uma clicked her tongue. "I can't let you go in there! I'm not going to risk losing you." She tightened her scarf around her shoulders. "I'll go."

I put my hand on her arm. "Granny Uma, you can't climb that high. You're going to have to let me go." I smiled even though my stomach squirmed like a thousand snakes. "I'll come back with Kaleb."

Granny Uma squinted up at the hollow and blew out all her breath. Giving in, she took off her necklace and put it around my neck. "Shake the seeds if you get in trouble. I will find a way to reach you even if you are swallowed up by the earth." She smiled too brightly.

The sky was a blaze of fire colours. I couldn't see the sun from behind the trees, but I knew that it was leaving the world behind. The bright moon was taking control of the sky and bringing its army of stars.

"The Switching Hour is here," Mally said. "You'd better be quick. We'll hoist you up!"

Mally and Granny Uma helped lift me, taking one of my legs on each shoulder. Tau bleated as I left him behind.

"I'll be back as quickly as I can!" I called down.

Holding the edge of the hollow, I pulled myself up and swung into the gap, landing inside the tree with a thump. The darkness was heart-quickening and stifling. The trunk absorbed all the light from outside. I listened for sounds, but it was quiet.

"Kaleb?" I whispered. The hollow was filled with what felt like leaves and dry grass, spongy and soft. The air was musty and hot.

"Kaleb! Where are you?" I called out. I crawled forward on my hands and knees, reaching out blindly.

I glanced over my shoulder. The hollow's mouth was still in sight, a small moon-shape of light. *How much further to go?* A skittering insect crawled over my hand and I flicked it away.

All I could hear was my own breathing as I crept further into the hollow. I tried not to think of the Dream Eater and where it might be.

I turned a corner in the tunnel, when I saw a faint glow.

I ran my hand over the grooves in the bark, following the tunnel. It was getting hotter. Sweat trickled down the side of my face.

The glow got brighter, when the tunnel suddenly opened up. My hair caught on bark as I carefully stood. The smell of dust and earth clogged my nose. I coughed, and the sound reverberated around the hollow space.

I was in the belly of the Dead Tree.

Chapter Twenty Four

"Where are you, small brother?"

I'd found the source of the strange glow. In the middle of the hollow there were lights, hovering in the air. *Glowbugs?* They were too round and too big to be the tiny insects.

I realized they weren't hovering.

The orbs were stuck, caught on string that spanned from one side of the hollow to the other. Glistening, silky string in an intricate pattern.

A huge web.

I counted ten glowing orbs caught in its strands.

My finger trembled as I gently reached out and touched one. It was warm and pulsed, as if it were alive.

"It can't be," I exhaled. The web shivered against my breath.

Ten glowbugs. *The ten missing children.*

I have to save them too. I plucked the glowbugs gently from the web, tucking them into my empty pocket, where Mama's stone and Kaleb's charcoal had been. The light glowed enough for me to see. I sat back down on the leaves.

"Where are you, small brother?"

I held my breath while I listened.

Something was breathing. Something alive and near.

There was someone in the hollow with me.

What if it's Badeko? My heart thudded against my throat.

I reached out around me, pushing away the leaves.

My fingers brushed over curly hair. Then warm skin. With trembling fingers, I gently laid my hand down and I felt the rise and fall of sleeping breath.

"Kaleb!" I sobbed.

I wrapped my arms around him and pulled him close. I pressed my cheek against his and breathed in. He still smelled of the mud from the lake. He smelled of kindling dust and hearth ash. He smelled of lavender from Granny Uma's home-made soap.

He smelled of home.

My small brother.

"Kaleb," I whispered. "It's me, Amaya!" I held his hand, wrapping my fingers around his. But he didn't wake up.

My breathing was jagged, too loud for the small space. "We need to get to Granny Uma," I said. "She'll know what to do!"

I shuffled down the narrow tunnel, carrying him towards the opening. The glow from my pocket cast warm light.

We were almost there! I could see the entrance to the outside grow larger with each step forward.

But our escape was blocked.

I wrapped my arms protectively around Kaleb, his skin clammy and cold.

As tall as me, the creature was almost camouflaged against the inside of the tree, its skin bark-coloured and swirling with patterns like the rings of a stump. Its body was long like a centipede. Its many legs twitched.

With eyes bright white, it stared at me from the mouth of the hollow.

Badeko.

The Dream Eater.

"I'm taking my brother home," I said as loud as

I could, which wasn't more than a whisper. "He belongs with his family."

The creature didn't blink or speak, but a picture began to form inside my mind.

What's happening? I shook my head but I couldn't stop the images from appearing.

It was the night that Mama had gone. I'd been swimming with the other children at the lake. I'd seen smoke rising from the direction of Town, but the first thing that told me something was wrong was the taste. The smoke hadn't tasted right on my tongue, not like smoke from stove wood, but burning thatch. Clay walls crumbling.

Faster than the others, I'd run home, but still it felt like it took an eternity to get there. I could feel I was running towards something bad. I knew Granny Uma was looking after Kaleb for the day. Mama had been so tired ... she was all alone.

I'd got to the path and Granny Uma had caught me in her arms, stopping me from running into the flames. I'd kicked out at her, wanting her to let me go, not caring if I hurt her. I didn't care about anyone then, not Granny Uma or Kaleb, who she carried in her arms.

Not a night goes by that I don't relive it all.

I could give those dreams to Badeko. Let it take away the fear and the fire. The pain of missing Mama. It hurt too much to keep it in my heart.

Give it all to Badeko.

Kaleb shuddered in my arms. It brought me back to the present.

My small brother. He needed me.

"Please," I begged the creature. "Give him back to me!"

I whispered into Kaleb's ear. "You have to wake up!"

The creature laughed, a sound like dry leaves crunching underfoot.

You didn't want him then, why do you want him now? The thought was finally unlocked. The terrible secret that I had hidden away, that I'd tried to cover up.

I hadn't wanted him. A sibling that would steal away Mama's attention and love. Who meant that Mama would only have one arm to wrap around me instead of two.

But afterwards it was his small arms that hugged me tight.

Kaleb always seemed to know when I was missing Mama.

I became aware of a song, with words I couldn't understand. The drumbeats tingled the hairs on my arms. I didn't know where it was coming from. The anger ebbed and I felt woozy. The light from the hollow got brighter and then dimmer, like time was stretching and shrinking. I was being pulled under the surface of sleep, diving into the dark part of the water. I could feel myself begin to go limp.

"No!" I gasped, my hold on Kaleb loosening.

I shook my head but I couldn't clear it. The song was seeping into my pores.

Everything slowed down. The air began to feel like water in my lungs. I reached up with a heavy arm and rattled the necklace but no sound came out. The seeds were silent.

Amaya. It was Mama's voice.

Mama! I tried to call out. But my words were like syrup, sticking to the roof of my mouth and gluing my lips together.

Remember who you are, I heard her say.

With careful fingers I reached into my pocket and grasped a familiar shape. I ran my thumb over the indent of my name.

Amaya. The name my mama had given me and engraved on to my tinderbox.

I placed Kaleb in the hollow of my lap, his head lolling against my knee, and brought the tinderbox out. I cracked it open and let the flint and steel fall into my palm, every movement agonizingly slow.

Trying to hold the steel against the flint felt like walking through water, the pull of it holding me back.

"Stop, or I'll set the hollow on fire!" I gurgled at the creature, my tongue tripping over the words. But the creature cackled its dry laugh. It knew I was afraid. *It doesn't think I'll do it.*

I struck the steel against the flint. It sparked. The song faltered, like a break in the rain.

I focused on calming my shaking hands. I struck the steel again. Sparks popped and vanished in the air.

The song grew to a roar. I was drowning in it.

With all my might, I struck the steel against the flint a third time. Sparks showered down on to the dry leaves and a puff of smoke appeared. Smoke turned into a flame that started to gobble up the dry nest in the hollow.

The song stopped but I was still frozen, trapped in the fiery nightmare. Flames grew higher. I heard screaming: Mama trapped inside the house. But this time it was me; I was the one trapped.

"Mama!" I cried out.

A small cough and I heard my name. "Maya."

I stared down into a face I knew so well. Black eyes studied my face, still confused by sleep.

"Kaleb!" I scooped him up and held him tight. He wrapped his arms around my neck. His quick heartbeat next to mine felt unreal. "Maya," he said again.

Shaking the last threads of the song out of my head, I searched around for the Dream Eater.

Where was Badeko?

Smoke filled the space around us. I wrapped my headscarf loosely around Kaleb's mouth, so he could breathe. He started to cry, the scarf muffling his howls. He pushed his face against my neck and I felt warm, sticky tears.

I inched away from the flames, trying not to inhale the smoke. The heat licked the back of my sweat-drenched tunic. Kaleb screamed in panic and clung so tightly to my neck that I struggled to breathe. The smoke started to sting my tongue.

The hollow. I leaned out, holding Kaleb tightly.

"Granny Uma!" I shouted down, tears streaming down my face from the smoke.

"Amaya!" I heard her shout back. I saw her

through the haze, her arms reaching up towards us.

I dangled my legs down, but I couldn't find a foothold. "I can't!" I coughed.

The tree was too smooth.

An ear-splitting crackle of fire drowned out her reply.

Kaleb clung on to my neck. He whimpered in my ear. I swung him around to face me, but he was stuck fast by fear.

"You have to let go!" I told him. "Granny Uma will catch you!"

Kaleb shook his head fiercely. He clung on tighter.

Against all my instincts, I tried to pry his small hands away from my neck. Although he resisted, I was stronger than him. I loosened his hands as he shrieked for me to stop, his face tight with terror.

"It's OK, I promise!" I cried.

"Granny Uma!" I roared down to the ground.

With relief, I saw a glimpse of two hands through the smoke.

It was Mally, standing on Granny Uma's shoulders.

I shuffled back and lay on my stomach, my legs reaching back into the hollow. Heat stung my bare feet but I didn't rush. Kaleb was quiet now and he seemed so small. I held him under his arms and he clamped hold of my wrists.

I kissed him on the forehead. He whimpered.

"Be brave, small brother."

He was heavier than he looked and my arms shook as I lowered him out of the hollow, towards Mally's reaching hands.

Kaleb swung below, looking up at me. Then I felt Mally grab hold of his waist and the weight of him was passed to her. I let go.

He disappeared into the smoke cloud.

For a moment everything was still. A bubble of silence, between relief and fear. Then I breathed in thick, choking smoke and I jumped into a crouch.

I peered over my shoulder. The inside of the tree was alight. Fire roared up from the throat of the hollow, chasing the smoke out. Pressure of the heat was like a pushing hand.

I clambered over the lip and shouted down. "I'm going to jump!" I knew I was too high, but I had no choice. It was break a leg or two or get roasted in the belly of the tree.

Just before I let go, I stared back into the hollow. Then I saw it.

Badeko writhed and twisted in the flames. A hissing escaped, like wet bark catching alight. I saw a net that shimmered in the light of the fire, before it vanished.

The Dream Eater crumbled into ash.

I swung my legs over the hollow's edge and let go.

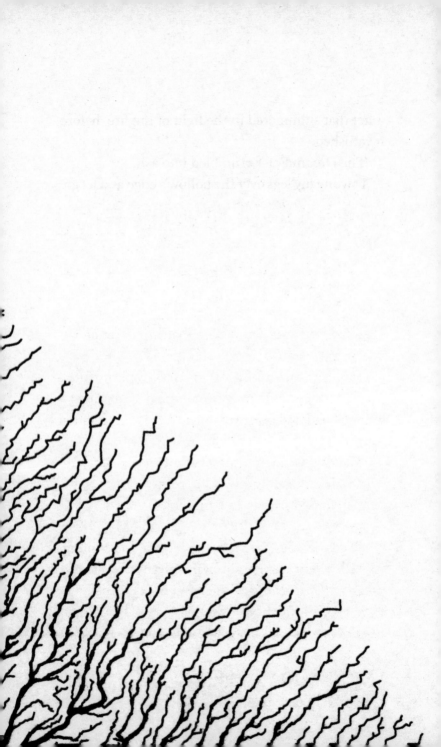

Chapter Twenty Five

"Time to go!"

The ground gave way and wrapped itself around me. I struggled against the folds.

Hands grabbed my arms and pulled me up into a stand. "It's just a blanket!" Mally said. She pulled it off my head and grinned at me. "We tried to soften your fall."

The bright moon turned her green eyes silver.

Granny Uma hugged me. "Are you hurt?"

"I'm fine." I scanned around frantically.

"Maya!"

There he was. Sitting on the ground and smiling. Tau curled up around him protectively. I swallowed again and again around the lump in my throat.

I scooped Kaleb up, inhaling his toddling smell deeply, that no mud or smoke could erase.

He laughed. His belly sound made me smile wide, even though my dry, chapped lips split and my sunburned skin hurt.

"I've missed that laugh." I giggled, which made Kaleb laugh louder.

Granny Uma kissed the top of his head. "You're going to need a nice, long bath when we get you home!" she murmured into his curls.

Mally tapped me on the shoulder. "We have to leave." She pointed at the Dead Tree. The flames were licking the outside of the hollow like a hungry tongue. I could feel the heat from here and flecks of ash rained down on us.

"Time to go!" Granny Uma shouted in agreement, as she clambered on to the cart and reached out for Kaleb. Reluctantly, I handed him over to her. This time he seemed to know that I would follow and he let go of me willingly. Granny Uma patted Zola on the backside and he set off at a trot, pulling the cart behind him.

"Come, Tau!" I called out, but he was already setting off, following the other two goats and checking over his shoulder for me to follow.

Almost as clear as day, the moon and stars illuminated our path, but the smoke from the Dead

Tree rose like clouds from the earth. Soon, they'd cover the light from the moon.

A hare darted across our path, its eyes white with fright. Then three small wild hogs came crashing out of some bushes, narrowly avoiding Tau's hooves. They fled in front of us, their skinny tails high in the air.

Mally glanced over her shoulder. "Oh no!" she gasped.

I turned to see the forest on fire.

"The blaze from the Dead Tree," Mally cried. "It's spread to the rest of the trees!"

The drought. It had made everything bone dry.

Granny Uma shouted. "We have to move! Now!"

Zola didn't need telling twice. He set off at a run, the cart rattling behind him, with Granny Uma and Kaleb bouncing on the seat. He was going too fast. I shouted out a warning, but it was too late. The cart careened into a burrow and stuck fast.

I ran over. Zola rattled the harness, throwing his horned head in the air. Granny Uma slid off the cart, Kaleb holding tight to her neck.

"The wheel is broken!" Mally wailed in dismay.

Granny Uma handed me Kaleb and he buried his face into my neck. The scarf I'd wrapped around his mouth had slipped and he coughed from the ash that spun from the sky.

Granny Uma kneeled down to the broken wheel. "I can fix this," she said.

"We don't have time to fix it!" Mally screamed, her eyes wild. She pointed frantically behind us.

We could see the flames, as the brittle trees and bushes erupted into fireballs. Embers twisted up into the air, tiny sparks turning into a blaze. Smoke billowed into the night sky.

Animals and birds passed us by, fleeing from the direction we'd come. Yellow-bellied snakes slipped through the dry grass and a short-tailed buck trotted quickly down the path. I saw a daggertooth pack fleeing, with pups in tow. Weaving birds shrieked and flew over our heads in a whirl of panicked feathers.

The fire had circled the clearing, leaving only a gap between two needle-thorn trees that were already starting to smoulder.

I turned back to the others.

"We have to go, now!" I yelled, clutching tightly on to Kaleb.

"We'll never make it!" Mally croaked, before a hacking cough took her voice away.

Ela and Zola skittered, their eyes rolling. They were going to bolt.

"Mally, climb on to Ela." I held on to Ela's horns, as Mally clambered up. "And Granny Uma," I yelled. "Climb on to Zola!"

She unhooked him from the cart and heaved herself up on to the goat's back, but as she reached down for Kaleb, Zola bolted. He ran towards the gap in the fire, with Granny Uma clinging on. I saw her try to climb off, but the goat was going too fast.

Once Zola had set off, Ela bolted too, with Mally on her back. Mally shouted at me, but her words were lost. The two goats with their riders were swallowed up by the smoke.

"Tau!" I shouted. A hard nudge on my shoulder and I turned around: Tau stood behind me, shaking with fear.

Kaleb clung on to me, as I clambered on to Tau's back.

"We have to make it!" I urged Tau to run. He careened towards the two needle-thorn trees, their brittle branches raised towards the smoke-filled sky.

As I watched in horror, the fire leaped from branch to branch like a leopard hunting prey, catching hold of the two needle-thorn trees. They erupted into flames.

A wall of fire closed the gap.

It was too late.

The heat pushed Tau back. Eyes streaming from the raining ash, I searched for another opening, a break in the flames, but the clearing was surrounded.

We were trapped.

Chapter Twenty Six

"Close your eyes and breathe in deep"

The world was on fire.

The heat of it pressed against us and scorched my lungs like I was breathing flames.

Ash poured down, covering Tau's coat and Kaleb's curls.

I jumped off Tau's back, holding Kaleb tight against my chest, and guided Tau to the middle of the clearing, as far away from the flames as I could. But the sand had already begun to burn under my feet, melting in the heat.

I instinctively reached for Mama's stone.

A glow illuminated my face.

"The glowbugs!"

I gently opened my pocket. Kaleb reached for the

light but I caught his hand and I wrapped my fingers around his.

"We need to let them go," I whispered to him. I cupped my hand into the pocket and opened my palm to the sky.

One by one, the glowbugs rose up into the air.

They floated up through the ash and smoke. Ten tiny glowbugs. We kept our eyes on them until they blinked out one by one. Too far away to see.

"At least we set them free." I tried to smile at Kaleb but my skin felt too tight. He watched me with his big eyes, too frightened and exhausted to cry. I wiped the grey ash from his wet cheeks and kissed him on his nose.

I didn't feel afraid. Not any more.

Tau placed his head on my shoulder and his nostrils flared. I could smell the bitter sweat-fear that clung to his coat. I leaned against him. I pressed my cheek against Kaleb's hot face.

Above the roar and crackle, I sang the bedtime rhyme.

> *Close your eyes and breathe in deep*
> *It's time for you to go to sleep*

Until the moon has gone to hide
I will be right by your side.

As soon as the words were out of my mouth, the ground trembled.

I wobbled as the shock travelled up my legs and into my body. Tau stumbled heavily against me, almost knocking me off my feet.

A bright flash tore the sky apart.

The ground rumbled again, making my bones shake. Kaleb wriggled in my arms. He pointed upwards.

"Maya!" he shrieked in my ear.

Clouds were coming from the south, devouring the sky. They gobbled up the stars like they were tiny fish.

A flash zigzagged across the clouds, followed by a *boom* that was so loud and close it echoed in my ears, making them sing.

I clutched on to Kaleb, who squealed at the sky.

"They're here," I gasped. "The rains have arrived!"

The moon disappeared into the belly of the storm. I breathed in the sharp smell of rain.

Clouds thundered towards us, rolling over the sky and unleashing a waterfall that poured towards the ground.

"Hold tight, Kaleb!" I wrapped my arms around him. Tau leaned in close to my side, tucking his horned head against my shoulder.

I held my breath.

Like the crack of a whip, the downpour hit.

We were engulfed by the storm; the rain hammered against my skin. I felt the weight of the sky on my shoulders. I laughed and water ran down my dry throat, making me cough out the ash and dust. The cold of the rain took my breath away, after the heat from the fire.

I searched for signs of fire that had surrounded us, but the rain was all I could see. Sheets of it, waves and waves of driving rain. A flood falling from the sky.

"Look, Kaleb!" I pointed at the forest.

Small spirals of smoke swirled in the driving rain, the only sign the fire had once roared.

I grabbed hold of Tau's collar and slowly we made our way towards the two needle-thorn trees, where Zola and Ela had bolted.

Rain stuck to Kaleb's eyelashes and bounced off his curly hair. He clapped his hands, sending out spikes of water. I washed off the dirt and sleep from his eyes as he squirmed in my arms, trying to catch the rain in his open palms.

The heavy rainfall pulled us towards the ground, making progress slow. I blinked through the downpour, searching for any signs of Granny Uma and Mally.

We reached the two trees. The blackened trunks still smouldered but there was no flicker of flames.

Once past the trees, I halted Tau.

"Granny Uma!" I shouted, the roar of the rain drowning out my voice.

I shivered. The rainclouds hid the light of the moon and stars.

Then out of the darkness, two shapes appeared.

Tau leaped forward, dragging me with him. The two shapes turned into Zola and Ela, Granny Uma and Mally still perched on their backs.

Granny Uma slid off Zola's back and ran towards us. She wrapped both Kaleb and me in a hug so fierce I couldn't help but laugh with the last bit of my breath.

"We're fine!" I answered her unspoken question.

Mally squeezed herself into the hug, before we all untangled ourselves.

With the mud oozing between my toes, I danced and jiggled Kaleb up and down on my hip as he tried to wriggle out of my arms. I wasn't ready to let him go just yet.

"Isn't it amazing!" Mally laughed. She spun around, streams of water flying from her fingertips. "The clouds have come home."

The rain eased off. Clouds still filled the sky, but they weren't as dark and thunderous. The moon peeked out from the darkest cloud and the world was illuminated in silver and grey. I looked over at Granny Uma.

She faced the sky, her eyes closed. Water ran down her cheeks like tears. Her hair was stuck to the lines of her face.

She looked like Mama.

"We can make it to the first refuge hut, it's not far," Mally said. Her feet were splashed with mud and her clothes soaked though. I'd never seen her so happy.

The moon was the brightest I'd ever seen it, as if the storm had washed away the dust from its face. Everything felt changed by the rain.

I let Tau carry Kaleb on his back, while I supported him with one arm. Kaleb leaned his head on my shoulder and nodded off to sleep as we followed the track, stomping through the mud, the rain still falling.

Chapter Twenty Seven

"The clouds have come home"

We made it to the refuge hut by the midnight moon. I was tired to my bones.

"Everyone inside!" Granny Uma ushered us all into the hut, goats and all. I carried Kaleb inside, where he squirmed to be let down immediately.

After checking the woodpile, Mally began building a fire and soon the room was full of warmth and light and the smell of wet goat.

Rain drummed on the tin roof, muffling our voices and blanketing us from the outside world. Steam soon rose from our clothes and hair, fogging up the windows.

Granny Uma stirred some oats into a pot of boiling water over the fire. The smell of porridge filled the room, making it feel like home.

Mally fed the goats and got them settled in a corner of the room.

I unwrapped Kaleb from the wool blanket and sat him closer to the fire. His cotton trousers and shirt were grubby and wet. Rummaging in my leather backpack, I pulled out Granny Uma's embroidered wool blanket from the cottage.

Thankfully it was still dry, and I wrapped Kaleb up. He yawned.

"You need to eat something before sleep, small brother!" I said, while I hung his clothes on one of the chairs to dry.

The room was warm, but we all huddled around the fire. Granny Uma passed out bowls of hot porridge. I spoon-fed Kaleb, laughing at his gawping mouth.

Mally wiped the porridge dribble off his chin with the edge of her dress. She giggled when he burped. "He's just like you."

I playfully elbowed her in the side. "Are you excited to meet your new sister?"

Mally's eyes lit up. "I can't wait."

After he'd eaten his fill of porridge, Kaleb fell asleep in my lap. I gazed down at his face, the firelight making his skin glow.

"Time for everyone to sleep," Granny Uma said

quietly. Carefully I stood up and settled Kaleb in the nearest bed, tucking him under the covers. I placed my hand gently on his chest, feeling the rise and fall of his sleeping breaths.

Before going to bed, there was one more thing to do. I went to check the door lock was firmly nestled into the latch. I checked it twice, pressing firmly down on the cold metal.

Mally had made a nest of the dry blankets near the fire. I curled up next to her.

I fell asleep to the song of the rain on the tin roof and Granny Uma's snoring.

The sun filtered through the window blinds when I opened my eyes, making golden stripes across the wooden walls of the hut. I yawned.

I hadn't dreamed at all last night.

Then I remembered.

"Kaleb!" I croaked. I untangled myself from the nest of blankets, Mally still sleeping soundly next to me.

In two steps, I was at the bed.

Kaleb lay arms outstretched, his eyes shut. I gently put my hand on his chest. It rose in time with his breathing. He didn't wake.

My heart hammered against my throat.

"Kaleb?" I whispered.

He opened his eyes. Blinked. Then looked up at me.

"Maya!" He laughed, stretching up his hands. I reached down and picked him up.

"You're getting heavy, small brother!" I groaned.

I carried him outside. The rain had stopped. I inhaled the sharp smell of wet earth and it sent a shiver through my bones. Tau nudged me out of the doorway and bounded on to the wet ground. He snuffled at the mud and dug a hole with his hoof, searching for roots. Kaleb squirmed and I set him down on the wooden deck.

The birds sang, flying from one tree to the next. Weaving birds danced along the branches and I caught the iridescent flash of a beetle bird's wing as it swooped at the flying termites that the rain had brought out of their underground nests.

Above me, the sky was dazzling blue, looking like the lake back home. But today, clouds skittered across its surface like white boats. More rain would be on the way.

The rainy season had finally arrived.

A smell of coffee wafted out of the open door. Granny Uma must be up.

Kaleb pulled at my tunic. "Maya!" he said, pointing in the direction of the forest.

I shaded my eyes from the rising sun.

A horse and rider appeared from the path that led out of the forest. The man was soaked through and his shoulders stooped. But his eyes widened when he saw me.

"Granny Uma!" I shouted through the open door. "There's someone coming!"

Mally peeked over my shoulder. She gave a whoop of delight and ran down the path.

The man jumped off the horse and flung his arms out when he saw her.

"Papa!" she shouted, her voice scattering the birds from the branches. He enveloped Mally into his arms, lifting her off her feet. She laughed and cried, as if she couldn't decide between the two.

Granny Uma joined me on the porch.

"About time he showed up!" She tutted but she was smiling.

Mally's papa put her down, but held her hand, as if he didn't want to let her go. Mally led him towards the cottage, full of chattering talk. I heard her ask about the baby, a look of worry in her eyes. Her papa smiled.

"She's been waiting to meet you," I heard him say.

Kaleb tugged at my hand, desperate to meet the new person. After a moment's hesitation, I let him go and watched him run on bouncy feet.

He's grown so big.
Mama would be so proud.

Epilogue

The day was at its brightest point. The sky was full of cloud, with more rain on its way. Bright green leaves grew on the trees and the grass sprouted from the wet earth, quicker than the goats could eat it. The land that was once turning to dust, now flourished with life.

In the middle of the forest, seedlings grew in a clearing, pushing through the layer of ash that surrounded the burned husk of a great Bao tree, its white bark crumbling.

Deep within the soil beneath the tree, a creature with lichen skin slept dreamlessly, waiting for when the land would be cracked and parched once more.

I dived into the water and twisted into the murky depths, Mally mimicking my movements. Her hair streamed behind her like lake-weeds.

I pointed at the bream. They moved as one, a silver shoal.

We let them glide past us, before we broke the surface at the same time, gasping and laughing.

"I've never seen so many fish!" Mally swiped her hair away from her eyes.

We floated on our backs, watching the clouds move across the sky. Some of them were tinged grey. I could smell the next storm on the air.

It had been a month of rain and the fields were green again.

The glowbugs had made it home to their families, ten toddling children. I'd gone with Granny Uma, as she had visited each family, checking over their toddling and prescribing herbal medicine for gaining back their strength after their long sleeps. Granny Uma said I'd make a great midwife one day. I'd felt a warm surge of happiness at the idea.

Mally's family had moved back to the Forest Settlement, back to the house that Mally loved. Mally was learning how to be a big sister, with my help.

"Girls, come back out!" Granny Uma shouted from the shore. "It's time for food."

"Race you there!" Mally set off splashing towards the shore. It hadn't taken her long to learn to swim, once I'd shown her how, but she still had a long way to go before she was quick – and quiet – enough to catch a fish. Right now, she looked like a wrathcat that had been thrown into the water by surprise, all wild red hair and flailing limbs, something I would never dare tell her.

I let her reach the shore before I spun through the water, enjoying the exhilarating rush as I glided just under the surface, my breath held and my eyes open, feeling like a bird through the sky.

Once out of the lake, I shook the water from my hair.

Mally plopped down on the blanket, next to her papa, her step-mama and baby Ada, in the shade of a needle-thorn tree. Granny Uma sat on a small wooden stool, intent on getting Kaleb to eat his goat's cheese sandwich.

"No!" Kaleb had learned a new word.

The warm sun quickly dried the water from my skin. The air was full of birds and their different songs, as they swooped for the crickets that buzzed in the long green grass.

I still missed Mama every day, but I wasn't scared of forgetting her. I didn't need a stone to remember who she was. *She will always be a part of me and Kaleb and Granny Uma.*

Tau bumped my hand gently with his soft nose. His horns were almost as big as Zola's now and he was careful not to hurt me.

"I haven't forgotten about you." I sat cross-legged on Granny Uma's blanket, that she'd spread out for us to sit on. I spooned some mash into a wooden bowl, placing it on the ground.

As he greedily ate it up, I scratched the spot between his ears. "Silly goat."

Acknowledgements

This story was written during a heatwave and it consumed me much like the heat did. *The Switching Hour* ate up my dreams and stole pieces from my childhood – my fears of the dark and the sound of rain on a tin roof. It devoured my thoughts and I would rattle on about wrathcats and daggertooth jackals to anyone who would listen. In the end, it took a whole crew of people to finally trap the tale within the pages of a book.

To the Scholastic team: Mary Jones, Bleddyn Sion, Penelope Daukes and Kate Graham for all your hard work on *The Switching Hour* and for preparing it for the world. To Lauren Fortune, thank you for being so patient and deftly guiding me through the editing process. You often saw the path through the forest when I was lost and wandering.

Thank you to Kelsey Buzzell for your gorgeous cover artwork. To see Amaya under the grasping hand of the tree for the first time was such a special moment, one I'll never forget.

Thank you to the tutors and class of 2017 on the MAWYP at Bath Spa University, especially Julia Green, Lucy Christopher and Janine Amos for your collective wisdom, encouragement and support. My dream of becoming an author was made real by all of you.

To Alice Sutherland-Hawes, who was the first to say yes. Your powerful belief in your author's stories, and stories yet untold, is what makes you not only an outstanding agent but a wonderful human being.

Thank you also to my online and offline writer friends, whose debuts are continuing to fly out into the world, connecting and captivating readers. I couldn't have survived the journey to publication without our shared moments of encouragement, humour and dread.

To my Bristol friends. You are all creative, brilliant people who are a constant inspiration.

Thank you to my parents, who are the kindest and bravest people. You brought me up to believe in adventure, wherever that might take me.

To my siblings, Josh, Beth, Hannah and Jordan. Each of you has a gift for making people feel accepted and loved. I'm so proud to be your big sister.

To my nana, the strongest soul I know, whose love of words and poetry I inherited.

To my partner, Josh. You make me happy even when I'm feeling sad and you're my shelter through the storms. This book wouldn't exist without you because I wouldn't have believed it possible.

To my two furry writing companions, Daisy and Jack. May you both be by my side for many stories to come.

And thank you, Reader; this story is now yours. May your dreams be full of warm heart and fierce strength.

Damaris Young studied on
the writing for young people MA
at Bath Spa University, where
she wrote her debut novel *The
Switching Hour*, whose fictional
setting was inspired by the
landscape and legends of Southern
Africa, where she spent her
childhood. She now lives in Bristol
with her partner and two dogs.

Find her on Twitter: @damarisyoung